a house full of women

elizabeth brewster

"A House Full of Women" first appeared in *Dalhousie Review.* "Essence of Marigold" and "The Letters" were originally published in *Fiddlehead.* "A Question of Style" was first published in *Saturday Night.*

The author wishes to thank the Canada Council for its assistance.

ISBN 0 88750 486 8 (hardcover)
ISBN 0 88750 487 6 (softcover)

Cover art by Maxwell Bates courtesy Canada Council Art Bank. Book design by Michael Macklem.

Printed in Canada

PUBLISHED IN CANADA BY OBERON PRESS

For Alice and Margaret

a house full of women

The Grandmother, the Mother and the Girl lived together in
a white house with green trimmings on Charlotte Street in
the little town of Milton. It was a smallish house, but comfortable enough. Downstairs, when you came in the front
door and turned to the right, there was a room that was a
combined parlour and dining-room, with a heavy dark
dining-table and chairs, a large rocking-chair for the Grandmother, and a couch, covered with flounced floral cretonne,
on which the Grandmother sometimes snoozed or the Girl
sometimes curled up to read or study. On the other side of

this room was the kitchen, with its wood-stove and its sturdy deal table covered with linoleum, off which they ate most of their meals unless there was company or it was somebody's birthday.

The Mother slept downstairs, in a room to the left of the hall stairs, facing the street, a room that might have been intended as a front parlour when the house was first built. The Girl and the Grandmother each had a room upstairs. The Grandmother's was next to the bathroom, so that she could reach it readily at night. Off the Grandmother's room was a tiny cubbyhole, used for storage, which could double if necessary as a guest-room. The Girl's room was in the front of the house, with a bow-window looking out onto the street. It was large and airy, with a double bed and a big closet, and the Grandmother sometimes told the Girl she was lucky to have it all to herself, now that her elder sister had left home to work.

There were no men in the house. The Father, who had been the Grandmother's Son, was dead. The Grandfather had died long before the Girl was born, and had not been of much account anyway. The Grandmother had for many years run a large boarding-house. After she had sold it, she had bought this smaller house, in which she had lived for a time with her son, her daughter-in-law and her two young granddaughters. Now the two women and the young girl were left in the house by themselves.

Milton, while the Girl was growing up, was a peaceful, rather dull little market town in the midst of farming country. There was a dairy, which boasted that it manufactured the best ice cream in the province, and a company that bottled ginger ale and the local mineral water. The streets were lined with elms and maples; the houses were trim and well painted, with clumps of flowers—pansies or bleeding heart—in the front and large vegetable gardens in the rear.

However, just at this point in time, when the Girl was

fifteen and was attending the local high school, the town was not as peaceful as usual. A War was in progress. Men were fighting and bombs were falling in Europe and Asia; and it was necessary for the men of the country, of the province and of Milton to go off and Save Democracy. Indeed, Milton was of special importance in the War. It became the site of a military camp, a camp that had a much larger population than that of the little town itself. The soldiers paraded through the streets, flaunting their uniforms. They overwhelmed the shops and eating places, or they prowled the sidewalks in search of girls, of whom there were not enough to go around.

Even in the house on Charlotte Street the War had its effect. The Mother cooked doughnuts in a pan of sizzling fat on top of the kitchen stove, and sold them fresh every day to the military canteen at the camp, although she herself never visited the camp. An old friend of her husband's, now in charge of the canteen, sent a man every afternoon to pick them up from her, or sometimes picked them up himself. The Grandmother fretted—she did not like the smell of doughnuts and cooking-grease—but could not object vehemently to her daughter-in-law's earning money from work that did not take her out of the house.

One morning in early September, after Stella, the Girl, had gone off to school, and when Maud Vining, the Mother, had already started on her morning's task of making doughnuts, the Grandmother came downstairs for her late, leisurely breakfast. When Maud heard her on the stairs, she hurried through the dining-room into the hall so that she could watch the Grandmother's slow, elaborate descent, walking backward and clutching the rails, her cane in one hand. She did not know what she could do if the Grandmother fell, but felt, somehow, that she could preserve her from falling by watching her.

7

The Grandmother, helped by the Mother, found her way to the kitchen, where she sat down at the far end of the deal table, awaiting her breakfast. As always, she looked, except for her massive size, like the imaginary ideal of an old lady: snowy hair, a round, china-pink face with a delicate skin, a scarcely wrinkled brow and a pink rosebud of a mouth, which could, however, tighten and harden when the owner did not get her way. She was dressed immaculately, as usual, wearing this morning a flowered cotton dress that the Mother had sewn, and a pink woollen shawl tucked comfortably around her shoulders. Every hair in its place, the Mother noted, conscious of her own hair, which (although of course she had combed it before breakfast) was now straggling wispily into her eyes. Already a spot of grease had splattered onto the apron she had put on to protect her house dress.

The Mother poured a cup of tea for the Grandmother from the teapot that always stood at the back of the wood-stove, and gave her the bowl of shredded-wheat and the toast and soft-boiled egg she liked for breakfast.

As the Grandmother sipped her tea, she turned over the pages of the weekly newspaper, which had arrived the afternoon before, and quoted bits of local news that the Mother had already read.

She's unusually friendly and chipper this morning, the Mother thought, looking warily at her mother-in-law.

The Grandmother began to read the ads, in search of bargains or information.

"Room rents are getting to be very high, aren't they, Maud?" she said at length, taking a sip of tea.

"Yes, I suppose they are. So many of the army wives are coming to be with their husbands, and rooms are all they can get."

The Grandmother crunched thoughtfully at her toast. "I wonder," she said, "if it wouldn't be the patriotic thing for me to rent a room."

8

The Mother looked up from turning the doughnuts with a fork and stared at her. "What room would you rent?" she asked. "There's only that poky little room off yours, and a person would have to be pretty hard-put for space to take it."

"Yes, of course it would be very small for an adult. But why couldn't Stella move into it? She's only a child and doesn't need so much room. Then I could rent her room to a soldier's wife. It would be patriotic. We shouldn't hold on to space when others need it."

Patriotic my foot, Maud thought. What she wants is the money.

"Stella's not a child," she said. "She's in high school now. She needs the room."

"She doesn't really need it," the Grandmother argued. "I never even had a room to myself when I was a girl, let alone a big room like that with a double bed. The little room next to me will be big enough for her to sleep in, and she studies down here most evenings anyway."

"I don't like strangers in the house, especially with a young girl like Stella growing up. How do we know what they'll be like or who they'll bring in?"

"Oh, Maud, you coddle Stella too much. Good for her to see a little life in the house. It'd only be one woman, and what harm could one soldier's wife—an officer's wife, maybe—do the girl? We'd look her over first, wouldn't we?"

"That little room's full of junk. Where are we to store it so that Stella can sleep there? And who's to do all the work? Is your high-and-mighty officer's wife going to do her own room? It's all I can do to get Stella to do it."

"Well, Maud, it was just an idea. I'm sorry you're so unpatriotic and selfish. I would have thought you'd have been willing to help some poor soldier's wife be near her husband so he wouldn't be chasing around after all the schoolgirls in town. And we could stand the money. But never mind."

She turned the page of the newspaper, and went on reading

9

silently to herself, but Maud looked at her warily. You could never tell what the old woman might be up to.

When next week's paper came to the house in the afternoon, the Grandmother, who was sitting in her big chair in the dining-room, managed to reach it before her daughter-in-law came in from the kitchen. "See, Maud," she said triumphantly, "they already have my ad in."

"What ad?" Maud asked blankly, standing at the kitchen door.

"My ad for the room, of course. Oh, Maud, don't look so mad. It's my own house—I do have a right to rent a room in it. Maybe no-one will come, anyway."

People did come, of course. The first was a middle-aged woman, an officer's wife, who looked at the room critically and decided that the clothes closet was not big enough and the furniture was old-fashioned without being antique. She could find something better, she thought. The second was a young girl from the country, a private's wife, who liked it very much indeed—such a lot of space, such a good view from the bow-window—but who could not afford as much money as the Grandmother was asking.

Finally a man came to view it, a Sergeant Rumble, who said he wanted it for his wife, who was moving to Milton shortly to be near him. He was a rotund, pompous man in his forties, with a military manner. He inspected the room carefully, sat down bouncingly on the bed to test its springs, tried the windows to make sure they would open without difficulty, peered into the closet, and said he thought the room would do nicely for his wife. He paid the Grandmother a month's rent in advance, and said his wife would be arriving next week from the city.

"Perhaps she won't like it when she comes," the Mother said hopefully to Stella. She expected a woman who would be

Sergeant Rumble's female counterpart, a sturdy, military-looking woman of 39 or 40, with definite opinions on what a room ought to be like.

Gladys Rumble, when she arrived, was something of a surprise. She was much younger than her husband, somewhere in her early twenties, a pretty girl with pale brown hair and light brown eyes. She was dressed becomingly but quietly, wore almost no makeup and seemed demure, almost prim, in manner. She appeared to be devoted to Sergeant Rumble, and Maud Vining decided she must be a fairly recent bride. "I can't see why she took him," she said to Stella. "I'd have thought she could do better, but love is blind."

Even though she had not wanted young Mrs. Rumble in the room, the Mother rather took to her at first. She was pleasant but not too pushy, took care of her own room, prepared her own breakfast without getting in other people's way and ate her other meals out of the house. She took a polite interest in the Grandmother's scrapbooks of Royalty, the Mother's cooking and the Girl's clothes and lessons. Sergeant Rumble was under foot more than the Mother liked; but, after all, it was good to see a married couple so devoted. If she had not been worried about Stella, she would have been well enough satisfied.

Stella, she thought, seemed tired and dispirited lately.

"Aren't you sleeping well, Stella?" she asked her one evening when Stella was helping her with the dishes. "Are you working too hard at school?"

"It's that little room, Mum," Stella said. "I can hear everything in Grandma's room, I'm so close. She snores and talks in her sleep. And I can hear things in the other room, too."

"What things, Stella?"

"Oh well, just the Rumbles laughing and making noises. Does he beat her, Mum, do you think?"

"Beat her? Oh, no, I can't imagine that. Just pull the covers up and try not to hear."

"I don't like that Sergeant Rumble," Stella told her mother another evening. "I was taking a bath last night, and I had closed the door but hadn't locked it because you know the lock doesn't work and nobody ever comes in. But Sergeant Rumble came in. He barged right in and stood there."

"I suppose he didn't know you were there, dear."

"Well, but he didn't rush out as soon as he saw me. He stood there and just looked, really stared at me. I almost had to tell him to leave."

"Poor Mrs. Rumble. He must have a wandering eye. We'll have to get the lock fixed, and don't you ever talk to him."

"I don't want to talk to him. That old man."

"I think they drink in their room," Stella said another time. "And there's another man, a friend of Sergeant Rumble's, who comes along with him."

"I don't think Gladys drinks," the Mother said. "I suppose he drinks with his friend, and she can't prevent him. So long as they don't get drunk and ruin the furniture. Your Grandma wouldn't like that—serve her right."

In October Stella caught the measles, and the Mother brought her down to her own room so that she wouldn't have to carry her meals upstairs to her. Gladys brought her portable radio downstairs for Stella, who was lying in the darkened room, unable to read. Stella thanked her, but turned the radio off when Gladys left the room. "The music hurts my ears, Mum," she said. "I'd rather just listen to the quiet."

When she was well, she did not move upstairs again to the little room. She continued to share her mother's bed, though she studied late on the couch in the dining-room. Sometimes she fell asleep there, the book she was reading dropped from her hand, and the Mother would come out and throw a blanket over her. At such times, looking at the thin young body and the pale face under the tangle of fair hair, the Mother would yearn to reach forward into the Girl's future and protect her from any danger that might be waiting there.

"Mum, I don't know whether I should tell you," Stella said to her mother one morning in November before she went to school. "That other man, Sergeant Rumble's friend, stayed with Mrs. Rumble overnight, and Sergeant Rumble wasn't there. I saw the man leaving this morning. He woke me up stumbling down the stairs, and I got up and turned on the light and saw him."

Maud looked at her in surprise. "Are you sure it wasn't Sergeant Rumble?" she asked carefully. "Do you know what you're saying, Stella? About Gladys?"

"Yes, I know what I'm saying. It wasn't Sergeant Rumble. I don't like that woman, Mum. She's sneaky."

"Well, she's your Grandmother's roomer. I can't get rid of her myself, but I'll speak to Grandma."

"I don't believe it, Maud," the old woman said angrily, when the Mother recounted Stella's discovery to her. "The girl's mistaken. You know what young girls are at that age. Full of fancies. Jealous of a pretty young married woman like Mrs. Rumble, maybe."

"You know that's not true. Stella's a very truthful girl. You're fonder of money than of your own granddaughter, that's what it is."

"Well, maybe I am. At least the woman's room is paid for. She can do what she likes in her own room, can't she?"

"Oh, so Stella and I don't pay rent, is that what you're saying? So who cooks your meals and cleans the house and washes your clothes for you? How do you think you'd manage if Stella and I walked out?"

"Well, Maud, keep your shirt on, don't go flying off the

handle all over the place. I know I need you, and you need a place to live too. Can't we get more proof before putting her out, though?"

"Well," Maud said to her husband's friend Harry, from the army canteen, when he came to pick up her doughnuts. "Who would ever have thought that Grandma Vining, who has always been so proper, would not care whether her roomer was entertaining other men besides her husband all night? Of course, I always thought Sergeant Rumble was too old for the girl, and I suppose she found that out after she married him. I'm sorry for her in a way."

"And how do you know she's married to Sergeant Rumble at all, Maud?" Harry asked, winking.

"What do you mean, Harry? Do you know anything about her?"

"Not much. But enough about Rumble to know he has a wife in Moncton, much around your age, and a couple of half-grown boys."

"Harry, have you known that all along? Why didn't you tell me?"

"Didn't know you'd want to know. Minding my own business. The girl's a common prostitute, to my mind. Easy enough to get rid of, if you want to, even if the old woman is being stubborn. A word here, a word there, and the girl will be arrested."

"I don't know if I want—still, I have to look after Stella, don't I? All this has been bad for Stella. But I'd rather she'd just leave town. Maybe if I spoke to her myself."

But she did not need to speak to her. That evening Gladys came in by herself, without either Sergeant Rumble or his friend. She stood in the door of the dining-room, her gaze taking in the Mother at her mending, the Grandmother with a crossword puzzle, Stella with her algebra text propped up in

14

front of her. She had changed her muted lipstick for a very bright shade.

"Well, Mrs. Vining," she said, "I'm sorry I'll have to be leaving tomorrow. My mother-in-law—Sergeant Rumble's mother, that is—is very sick and wants me to be with her. She's a lovely lady, just like a real mother to me, and I want to help her out. I think it may be a long sickness, so you'd better rent the room to someone else."

The Grandmother looked up from her crossword, startled. The Mother was silent for a moment. (She knows we know, she thought. The man must've told her Stella turned on the light. Or did Harry see that she was warned?) "I'm sorry to hear that, Mrs. Rumble," she said. "We'll miss you, and so will the Sergeant, I'm sure, but we all have to take care of our own when they need us, don't we?"

"Yes, we do. Well, I'll be taking that early-morning train, and I guess the rent's all paid, so I don't need to see you again. Thanks for everything. And good luck with your lessons, Stella."

Stella looked up without answering. Maud could not guess what her thoughts might be.

In the morning the Mother and Stella ate breakfast together. Gladys had already left for the station. The Grandmother was not yet up.

"Well, she had her good qualities, in spite of everything," Maud said. "She was always neat and tidy, and had a pleasant smile."

"She always had very pretty dressing-gowns," Stella said. And sighed.

The Mother glanced at her. "Handsome is as handsome does," she said vaguely. "I'm glad to see the last of her, whatever her good qualities."

Shortly before Christmas the Mother met Sergeant Rumble

15

and his wife on the street. His real wife, that is. A stout woman with a strong jaw. Sergeant Rumble did not recognize Maud, or at any rate did not appear to.

In the New Year Sergeant Rumble and his friend and most of the men in the camp were sent overseas. A new group of soldiers invaded the town. One or two of them knocked at the door of the house on Charlotte Street, inquiring about rooms for their wives, but the Grandmother refused to rent the room again. The Mother moved upstairs to the room where Gladys had slept and left the downstairs room for Stella. The room, she explained to herself, seemed hardly suitable for a young girl any longer. And in fact it was the room she had slept in during her marriage, although she had moved out of it when she became a widow.

Getting ready for bed, standing in front of the old gilt-framed mirror in her faded navy blue dressing-gown, brushing her greying hair, she wondered where Gladys was now. And, stretched out in the big double bed, where Gladys had entertained Sergeant Rumble and his friend, and where she herself had once slept with her own husband, she thought about Gladys, and the real Mrs. Rumble, and Gladys' invented mother-in-law, and her own mother-in-law, and Stella, asleep in the room just under her. Why, she wondered, were some women's lives so different from other women's lives? But you could never answer that.

The room was cold. It must be the coldest room in the house, and something was wrong with the furnace again. She must see about that in the morning. Meanwhile, she pulled the blankets tight around her and shivered.

16

essence of marigold

I am sitting here at my dining-room table staring at a large
yellow marigold that I bought this morning in the Farmers'
Market. Only ten cents, but beautiful and crinkly, undeniably real. Marigolds have almost no scent, it's true, but if I
press my nose right up against it, this one gives off a faint
spicy odour, like some kind of kitchen herb. Not at all sweet,
mildly medicinal in fact, but pleasant. I have put it in a little
brown pottery vase and set it in the centre of the table.
Geraniums also: a double red geranium in a tin container.
Exactly the shade of red geranium my mother would have

17

liked.

Should I paint one of them? A still life, say—marigold and transistor radio? Geranium on window-sill, with prairie city beyond it? (The geranium must stay in the tin container, which must not be camouflaged in any way.) No. I don't feel like painting them. I have painted flowers from time to time (pale narcissi in a brown pot set against a blue background; also those deep red, semi-purplish gladioli now framed on my living-room wall). I think I was trying to hold on to them, but these flowers I intend to let go. I couldn't catch their scent, anyway. (The geranium, some people would say, has no scent. Except in the leaves.) And anyhow I have gone on to other things than flowers. Prairie landscapes. Crowd scenes. I am a good painter. Maybe not great, but good. Too conscientious, maybe? Not experimental enough? A failure in imagination? My fans (and I have fans, bless them) wouldn't say so. They think of me as a female prairie Alex Colville—or maybe that Alex Colville is a male Maritime Daisy Lister. If I don't have quite Colville's reputation, I have the excuse that I'm a few years younger.

I'm a few years younger than Marguerite Chrystal, too. An admirable painter, though unlike Alex Colville. The magic without the realism. If she painted the marigold, she would paint its essence. One might think of the heart of the sun, or of the ruffled flight of a ballerina. (I have a fleeting image of a ballerina as I might paint her: I would concentrate, I think, on the muscles. Ballerinas are really tough ladies. I like that combination of toughness and grace.)

Marguerite is in my mind just now because she has painted my portrait. Oh, not in oils. No, she has written a short story about me. (Marguerite, unfairly, has several talents.) She told me about this story, said she would send me a copy, but forgot to. I ran across it yesterday in the public library, stood reading it at the magazine rack, trying to decide in my mind whether I liked it, as the ballet dancer might stand in front of my portrait of her, objecting to the prominence of her muscles. Has she caught my essence, I wonder?

Really, though, the story is not so much about me as it is about memory. Here are two women, two painters, who have quite different memories of the occasion when they met. Which is telling the truth? Are there two truths?

I have a diary dating from the time I met Marguerite. I have a bundle of letters from her. (She has forgotten she wrote me.) I have clippings about exhibitions, a few sketches. I could look them up, I could document this account, but I don't intend to this time. I'll try to get at the essence.

I arrived in Saskatoon by myself on the train that day, the day I was to collect the prize. (I insist that I arrived by myself, although Marguerite is equally certain that my parents came with me.) My certainty springs from the fact that my arrival by myself was a triumph. I was my parents' only child and too much protected. I had never been separated from my mother for more than a day. On this occasion, however, I had argued (successfully) that I was perfectly able to look after myself. After all, I was almost seventeen. (Marguerite remembers me as younger, a plump, composed child, perhaps twelve, fourteen at most. I was, in fact, rather thin, if not scrawny, and not at all composed.) The trip to Saskatoon from Kasoba was not a difficult one, although rather long, and I was to be met at the railway station by one of the local artists, a Mrs. Curtis, who was putting me up in her house. Lucky that Mrs. Curtis made that offer. If I had been staying at an hotel, for instance, my parents would not have felt I should be alone. But they could not have afforded a good hotel, either for themselves or for me. Once before, I had won a prize for a watercolour, but had not been able to come. If I had I'd have spent all my prize money.

Now, as the train chugged its way through the autumn fields, stopping here and there at small prairie towns, I was torn between delight and fear. I was free, and I was about to encounter the unknown. I ate the egg sandwiches and solid doughnuts that my mother had packed for my lunch, half in a delightful daydream, half in nervous fear that something would go wrong.

Saskatoon station. Much larger than the station at Kasoba, and I have never been here before. I am wearing a navy-blue suit, handed down to me by a cousin in Ontario who is a year or so older than I am. I hate it, but am lucky to have it. Anyhow, I have told Mrs. Curtis that I will be wearing this navy-blue suit. I have no idea what she will be wearing or what she will look like. For some reason I imagine her with white hair, fat like the eldest of my aunts.

While I stand there uncertainly, there rushes up to me a trim little woman in a smart dress—I can't describe it, I just know it is smart—with her coat flung over her shoulders. Her hair is piled up on top of her head in an auburn mass, from which a few wisps have escaped. She is holding a chubby little boy, three or four years old, by the hand. They look as if they have both been running.

"Daisy Lister?" she gasps. "I'm Bea Curtis."

Mrs. Curtis takes charge of me immediately. I am whisked, with my little battered suitcase (my mother's little battered suitcase, that is) out of the station and into a taxi. Taxis are rather outside the range of my experience. In Kasoba everything is within walking distance. I walk to school every day; my father walks to the drugstore where he works for his small wartime salary; my parents and I walk to church together on Sundays. Sometimes one of my uncles who is better off than my father takes us for a drive in his car, but not too often. Mrs. Curtis and the little boy (Binker, he is called) and I all sit together in the back seat of the taxi. I am delighted with Saskatoon. It has trees and a river, as Kasoba hasn't, and a huge hotel that looks like a castle. "Pretty river," Mrs. Curtis says abstractedly to Binker.

20

I think that she is speaking to me, and say "Yes" a little too fervently. She looks at me with surprise, and I turn a bright pink (I feel the blood rushing into my face) and lapse into silence.

I am to collect the prize for my watercolour that evening, at a meeting of the Group. The Group is trying to encourage talent in improbable places like Kasoba. That is why I am here. It is Marguerite who has written to me before, and I rather wish I could have stayed with her, but she does not have room. She is a genuine artist (I suspect that Mrs. Curtis isn't) and is living in some hand-to-mouth artistic way in a single room.

Mrs. Curtis settles me into a trim little room in her trim little house. She looks me over thoughtfully. There is time, she thinks, to put a few pin curls in my hair. What do I plan to wear? I have a new dress, bought especially for the occasion, a green flowered dress with a fussy lace collar. I like it myself, and in Kasoba it seemed right, but I see through Mrs. Curtis' eyes that it is all wrong. Perhaps without the lace? It was the lace that I had especially liked, but Mrs. Curtis persuades me (tactfully, tactfully) to allow her to take the collar off while I am having a nap before dinner. Not that I do have a nap before dinner. (Supper, we called it in Kasoba.)

At dinner, I meet Mr. Curtis, who is a business man in the city, rather older than Mrs. Curtis and beginning to go bald. He is a friendly man. "I like your painting, Daisy," he says. "I don't know much about art—Bea's the artist around here— but I thought you should get the prize. That field of black-eyed Susans—I do like that."

I see that his opinion isn't to be taken seriously, but he is kind. I like him, as I like Mrs. Curtis. I am intimidated, however, by the fact that there is a maid who waits on the table and even wears a uniform. Nobody that I know in

21

Kasoba has a maid. I find it difficult to talk in the presence of somebody who is in the room but not part of the company. Anyhow, it is hard for me to keep my mind on dinner or on Mr. and Mrs. Curtis. I am thinking of the evening to come, of meeting Marguerite, of being presented with my prize.

The meeting that night is in an artist's studio (Marguerite and I agree on that). A big attic room without much furniture; burlap curtains at the windows; canvases propped against walls. There are some poets present as well as the painters. (I remember a dentist who told me he wrote a sonnet a day and kept his writings in a barrel.) Marguerite has not yet arrived when Mrs. Curtis and I come in. The studio is like a stage waiting for its leading lady. (Though surely I am the leading lady for that evening, the Promising Young Artist from out there in Kasoba?) There is a handsome young man present with dark hair and brown eyes who seems to me the leading man and who attaches himself to Marguerite as soon as she comes in.

2

It is morning again (Sunday morning), and I look once more at my marigold and the geranium, which have survived the night very well. The marigold has perceptibly more scent today than yesterday. A scent like that of the marigolds in my mother's garden, although hers were the tiny button marigolds rather than large ones like this. There was a thunderstorm last night—one of those thorough-going prairie storms—and the sky is still sullen: but patches of blue show through the clouds, and I hear crows cawing. I drink a cup of coffee and read over what I have written. Why, I wonder, do I delay so long about actually bringing Marguerite onto the scene? Is it because I am afraid I can't possibly paint her essence? Her essence has always seemed to me a mystery, untouchable. I, on the other hand, am not at all mysterious. I have often painted my own portrait, not so much from any great narcissism as from the realization that I look like so many other people I know. My mother told me early on, "You may be talented, but that doesn't make you better than other people." I tend to agree with her: painters, poets, millionaires may have some special ability to handle paints or words or money, but we are really only ordinary people with one highly developed skill, like jugglers or *cordon bleu* chefs.

Nevertheless, I didn't think Marguerite was ordinary. I didn't expect her to be ordinary. There was something extraordinary about her letters, even their appearance on the page. Her handwriting was excited and angular, with high loops that reminded me of bird-wings, quite unlike my own careful schoolgirlish hand. Her sentences were breathless, flying in all directions at once. On the margins there were often quick sketches of creatures on the wing, fabulous birds, butterflies, sometimes weirdly distorted and frightening, but always strangely beautiful.

When I imagined her—created an image of her to go with the letters—I imagined someone small and quick and birdlike, with piercing bright eyes. I saw her in my mind dancing in bare feet with peacock plumes in her hair. The real Marguerite wasn't like that. She was handsome, though—handsome rather than beautiful, I think—a tall, statuesque young woman somewhere in her twenties. She was dark (there I had guessed right) and glowed rather, I fancied, like those spikes of crimson gladioli that I painted later with their purple shadows. I was—and yet was not—disappointed, and stood there readjusting my vision of her while she bent over me (she was so much taller than I). I caught a surprised expression also on her face. "You don't look the way I imagined you," she said, but did not elaborate, and I fancied that she must be disappointed, that she had possibly invented someone more flower-like as the painter of those black-eyed

Susans and red lilies. Years later, she told me, "It was your age. I hadn't expected someone quite so young, a mere child."

"I wasn't a mere child," I said indignantly, remembering my seventeen years, from which she had so absurdly subtracted. (At that point she remembered me as having been only ten. She almost fancied having met me with a doll in my arms.)

Still, I suppose I did seem younger than my age. My parents had babied me, and I was a shy little person without many friends. I had not yet been out with a boy. Even for Kasoba, I guess I was backward. There is some truth, then, in her memory of me as being a mere child. A partial truth.

As far as the presentation with the prize is concerned, I don't remember it at all. I suppose the prize was a cheque. I went home afterwards with money, which I spent rather foolishly in my mother's opinion. (I also sold the painting of black-eyed Susans to Mr. Curtis, who wanted it for his office. My first sale.) I don't remember who handed me the prize. Marguerite, maybe? Mrs. Curtis? Some man or other, more likely. I envisage someone older and dimmer. Marguerite remembers me as very composed at the time of the presentation, pleased but unimpressed. Possibly. She also has distinct memories of both my parents and of their reactions. Quite untrue, of course. My parents were not there. As I keep insisting.

After the presentation, the meeting turned into a party. There were drinks, cocktails possibly, beer possibly. I think I had a ginger ale. My parents, I knew, would not have approved my drinking anything stronger. Perhaps indeed ginger ale was all I was offered.

I sat, I remember, next to Marguerite and the dark young man. I don't remember his name, but I fancy (or fancied) that he and Marguerite were in love. I thought that Marguerite was terribly sophisticated, sitting there with her drink and her cigarette, from which she blew elaborate smoke rings.

They talked, she and the dark young man, about painting, about poetry, about the pronunciation of the word "extraordinary." (Why do I remember that?) Marguerite leaned forward intently. She was rapt, caught up in the presence of the dark young man. She quoted Edna St. Vincent Millay, "Euclid alone has gazed on beauty bare." She quoted again, "Only until this cigarette is ended." (Does she remember quoting Millay? Probably not. A poet who has become unfashionable. The dark young man quoted W. H. Auden in return. I fell in love a little, I think, with both Marguerite and the dark young man. And more deeply in love than I had been before with painting.

That, of course, was the essence. That was what she left out of her story, because she didn't know it. How could she?

I couldn't sleep that night, I remember. I lay awake in the little room in Mrs. Curtis' house, reconstructing the dimly lit studio, inwardly posing Marguerite and the dark young man. I could have painted them. In fact I sketched them together the next day on the back of an envelope in my purse, as I was going home on the train. Maybe the envelope that contained my cheque, I don't know. I never saw the dark young man again (he is dead now, I think) and I did not see Marguerite for over twenty years.

That is not to say, however, that she disappeared from my life. Far from it. There were in the early years her letters, which came from time to time from different cities, from Montreal, Toronto, Vancouver. She learned to type, and her letters came now typed on yellow paper, but still rapid, exclamatory, decorated with those marginal flying creatures. Marguerite doesn't remember the letters. She thinks I have kept them because of some strange passion for documentation —if indeed I have kept them. She wavers between thinking I keep letters, diaries, documents, old sketches because I am unimaginative and need them to lean on, and that other (disquieting?) possibility that I haven't kept them at all, or that I am inventing letters that perhaps never even existed. It's strange that she isn't able to imagine why I kept them, or why I might invent them if I hadn't received them. She can imagine the phoenix, the unicorn, the marriage of heaven and hell, the day of judgment. She can even imagine my parents, though she hasn't got them quite right. (My father didn't have rough, callused hands, as she thinks. he had beautiful hands of which he was rather proud. It's a detail, but important, as physical details so often are.) In spite of her ability to imagine (and I always told her she was the imaginative one) she can't imagine why I kept her letters. I marvel.

We had lost track of each other for a while when I wrote to her again, that year I was home with a back injury. I had been thrown from a horse, and spent six months or so in a cast recovering back home in Kasoba, with my mother fussing over me. A dull space of time, but I did a lot of work that year. I was beginning to get some reputation by then—I suppose that's why I thought I could write her again. She invited me to visit her in Vancouver if I ever reached there: but by the time I went to Vancouver she was somewhere else, New York I think, and I lost track of her again.

I seemed always to be arriving in places after Marguerite had left. Montreal, Toronto, Vancouver, London, Paris. I spent a year in Boston; she spent a year in New York. We shared a number of the same friends at different times. We won the same awards for different reasons. For a short time, in Vancouver, I even had the same lover as Marguerite had had. Not for long, though. I felt, perhaps unreasonably, that comparisons were being made, and looked elsewhere.

It's hard to say what Marguerite meant to me—the idea of Marguerite, that is to say. A Muse, an ideal? Perhaps. A friend, an older sister, a rival? All of those. A model? Definitely not. Influences work in peculiar ways, as I am tempted to tell the young person who is doing a thesis on my

26

work. One may be influenced to go in the same direction or in the opposite direction. If Marguerite insists on painting the phoenix or the day of judgment, I must paint marigolds or geraniums. Or if I paint the phoenix, I must demonstrate that he flies like a crow, or the day of judgment resembles a farm auction in the Depression. I can't, or won't, paint like Marguerite any more than I would dress like Marguerite or talk like Marguerite. I am inexorably, stubbornly myself. Marguerite doesn't need to be stubborn. It has never occurred to her to be anyone but herself. She never kept my letters and doesn't even remember them, or thinks she doesn't. But where has she got that picture of my parents, inaccurate though it is, except from the letters and sketches I sent her?

Marguerite was out of the country for a number of years, in Athens, in Calcutta, in Rio de Janeiro. Her paintings showed the effects of that restless wandering. During that time I came home, after my parents' deaths, to the prairie, dug myself in, settled down, became that painter whose "deliberate ordinariness elevated to the level of myth" pleased some art critics, though definitely not all. During the last ten years or so, since she came back to Ottawa, I have seen Marguerite a number of times. We have visited each other's exhibitions, admire each other's work as much as sisters ever admire each other's work.

"I always knew we would see each other again," she tells me when I visit her that first time in Ottawa. "People who are important to each other always recur in each other's lives. It's part of the pattern."

I see that she envisages us in a tapestry woven by some great celestial artist. She has made tea for me; we drink it ceremoniously, a communion. I look at her doubtfully over the teacup. She has been important to me, oddly, all these years, but if I have been important to her, I am trying to imagine how.

27

a question of style

I met Lord Peake—Jeremy Peake, First Baron Peake of Tantramar, to give him his official name and dignity—in the summer of 1949, just after I had won a Peake Overseas Scholarship to the University of London. I was visiting my parents in Sackville when Lord Peake arrived there. He had decided to spend a month in New Brunswick, where he had grown up, and had bought rather a handsome old house in Sackville for his visit. It was typical of him that he could not be satisfied with merely renting a furnished house for that short period, but must buy one, and have it totally redecorated.

The first Baron Peake of Tantramar would not hold court in rented rooms. It was showing off, of course; and a man of as much wealth but less ostentation might have stayed quite comfortably in a few rooms at the local inn. Yet I could not help feeling a grudging admiration for the gesture, which, after all, showed a sense of style.

I had been invited (or commanded) by Lord Peake's secretary to call at the house early one afternoon. I arrived promptly at the appointed time, wearing a carefully quiet summer dress that I thought suitable for meeting a distinguished older man. I was shown first into a small office and then, after a few minutes of waiting, into a larger office that was, however, practical rather than imposing. It had a sizeable desk, an array of bookshelves filled with the sort of standard collections that tell nothing about the owner, and a clutter of current newspapers and magazines. Above the desk was a painting of the Tantramar marshes by a local artist— quite a good painting. Either Lord Peake or someone who worked for him had some taste in this sort of thing.

I wondered if I was to be led into yet a further sanctuary, and sat down to wait. What would Lord Peake look like in the flesh, I wondered? I had seen pictures of him now and then in the newspapers over the past ten years or so. When I had been going to high school in Sackville, he had been a member of Churchill's cabinet and very active in the war effort. He was at that time Sir Jeremy Peake, not yet the first Baron Peake. I tried now to recall what he looked like in these pictures. A little man, I seemed to remember, who could not be placed as either young or old. He often wore a hat, slightly tilted over one eye. Could he be bald? No, there were some pictures without the hat. He was not fat, as far as I could recall; but neither was he thin. A mediocrity, I might have thought except that there was something about him, even in the newspaper pictures. Something about his mouth, the jut of his chin. Something denoting energy, shrewdness, possibly stubbornness. There was certainly eagerness—or was it impatience?—in the way he leaned forward, fronting the camera. He was always in the foreground, never the background, even though he was usually in the company of royalty or prime ministers.

While I was passing these mental pictures before my eyes, a door opened and Lord Peake entered, carrying a file folder from which he was reading. I recognized him at once, but found him, in spite of his shortness, more imposing than I had expected. The magnetism of his eyes, perhaps, or something determined and cocky about his walk.

I stood up to greet him, and he waved a hand in my direction as he proceeded, still reading, to his desk. "Remarkable," he said at length, turning toward me. "Remarkable." I did not know what was remarkable, and stood stupidly staring at him.

At length he said to me, indicating a chair, "Sit down, Miss Ridley. You do have a truly remarkable academic record."

I murmured in some embarrassment that I was glad he thought so. I knew that he himself had not bothered to complete the work for his university degree, and somehow doubted whether he was truly impressed by those high grades and academic prizes that were the result of rather grim industry on my part. Yet we were not unlike in our effort to escape from the poverty of small-town New Brunswick; and I could imagine that neither of us had been much loved by those schoolfellows we had been so eager to surpass in one way or another.

"Speak up, girl," Lord Peake said. "I don't hear you."

I was startled. Was Lord Peake deaf? Nobody had told me he was; but he must be in his middle sixties, older than my father, and my father was hard of hearing. However, I could always make my father hear when I wanted to. I raised my voice and repeated my previous words.

"This essay of yours," he continued, "has style. Style is

something I recognize, Lorna my girl, style and sincerity."

The essay had been required as part of the application for the Peake Scholarship, and his compliment on it filled me with mixed emotions. The application had asked the question, "Why do you want this scholarship?" I had answered partly out of my own feelings, partly with a view to what Lord Peake might expect and want. I knew that Lord Peake was a passionate supporter of the Imperial connection, that the professed aim of his graduate scholarships was to give a group of young Canadians a chance to study in the heart of the Empire. I might not myself feel entirely comfortable with words like "Empire" and "Imperial." Nevertheless, England was a romantic daydream to me. So my essay both was, and wasn't, sincere. Had Lord Peake detected insincerity, I wondered?

And was Lord Peake himself sincere now? I am easily flattered. I like to be praised. And yet I always find myself examining praise with suspicion. Did Lord Peake really like my essay? And if his praise was genuine, was it worth anything? He was a millionaire and a politician, not a literary critic. Still, he, or someone who knew his tastes, had chosen that very creditable painting. He was an owner of newspapers, an orator who was capable of turning a phrase if it suited him. His own style was popular, but it was undeniably style.

"And what does your father do, Lorna?" he asked.

I felt on safer ground. "He works in the stove foundry here in Sackville," I said. "He's worked there all his life."

"Ah, in the stove foundry. Well, my father was a butcher. Did you know that, eh, my girl?"

"Yes, I knew that," I said, taking care to keep my voice loud and firm. (His father had, in fact, been a butcher's assistant in the neighbouring town of Dorchester, as I had been told by an old acquaintance of his. "This 'Jeremy' business is pure fancy," the man had said. "He's Jeremiah Peake, and his father was Ezekiel Peake, who worked in Gabe Todd's butcher shop, and was a Deacon in the Reformed Baptist Church. They lived over the other side of the railway tracks.")

"Well, you're not in the stove foundry and I'm not behind a counter. We've both succeeded, haven't we, Lorna?"

"I hope so. It'll be a long time before I know," I said.

"Well, you have a good start. Anyone who's ambitious enough can succeed. Use your brains. Use your initiative. Don't be timid. Don't give up. And speak up, girl, speak up."

It was a short interview. We parted on fairly amicable terms, although by the end of the interview we were both shouting at each other.

"I'll see you in England in September," he said as I left. I was once more surprised. So he continued to see his scholar-ship winners, did he? Or was this a promise—or a threat—he was making without intending to keep it?

Later, when I was talking to Christina Partridge, the only other woman who had won a Peake Scholarship that year, she asked me, "How was your interview with Lord Peake?"

"All right, I guess," I answered, "but I didn't know he was deaf."

"Deaf? He isn't deaf."

"Well, he kept asking me to speak up, and I did. I thought he must have trouble hearing."

"He must've thought you spoke too low, that's all. Of course he wouldn't have to tell me to speak up." Chrissie, who was older than I, was a large, bluff girl who had been in the CWAC's—the Canadian Women's Army Corps—during the War. To her, he had almost whispered.

Chrissie and I, as well as the five men who had also won the Peake scholarship, two of them accompanied by wives, sailed from Montreal early in September for England. We were interviewed, on the morning of our departure, by a reporter who seemed annoyed with me because I did not sound excited enough to please him. "Can't you say something enthusiastic?" he asked. "It would be a better story if you were more excited."

I was, in fact, enormously excited; but I was determined to appear calm and phlegmatic. I was not going to look a fool to please any reporter. Chrissie expressed enthusiasm, of course; but then she had been in Britain during the War, and could not be expected to view the trip as such a great adventure. The reporter had counted on me to provide human interest for his story, and I had disappointed him. Perhaps I also disappointed Lord Peake.

Lord Peake's influence reached us as soon as we disembarked from the ship. We were met at Liverpool by one of his employees, a Mr. Collop, a bald, bushy-browed, businesslike man, who took charge of us, provided us each with an envelope containing some ready cash, whisked us ahead of many of the other passengers in the queues for immigration and customs, and shepherded us onto the train for London. In the compartment that Chrissie and I shared with two of the young men, we were provided with an array of English magazines and newspapers—including, of course, Lord Peake's own newspaper, the *Clarion* —and were handed a large basket of fruit. It was still near enough to the War that we had all experienced shortages of oranges and bananas, and regarded the lavish display of them with respect. Chrissie picked up the card from the top of the basket. "With the compliments of Peake," she read. "He's written it himself." And she displayed the card, written in Lord Peake's large, somewhat grandiloquent hand.

"The Lord will provide," Paddy Newcome said, taking the card and peering at it before returning it to Chrissie.

In London, we separated to our different destinations. Lord

33

Peake, or Mr. Collop acting for Lord Peake, had deliberately established us in different parts of the city, so that we were thrown on our own devices. However, we exchanged addresses and telephone numbers, and in the first days, at any rate, managed to keep in touch with one another. Chrissie and I especially became quite friendly.

We had been in London less than a week when Lord Peake entertained us for the first time. As the term had not yet started, I was still living in the small, shabbily respectable hotel in South Kensington where I had been placed by Mr. Collop, and was gradually finding my way around London by bus and tube. Every morning I set out on foot with my little blue atlas of the city in my hand, and every evening I returned to the hotel so tired that I had only enough energy to sit in my chair in my dark little room, feeding pennies to the gas meter when the room became chilly, and writing long letters home, full of the marvels of the Victoria and Albert, the British Museum, Carlyle's house, Madame Tussaud's establishment and all the parks. Later in the autumn, London would be dark and foggy, but these September days were warm, sunny and mellow; and I had rarely been happier (in spite of some loneliness) than I was on a fine afternoon in London, strolling in Hyde Park or Kensington Gardens or Battersea, in a setting that appeared almost rural, and yet was (I thought) the crossroads of the world.

It was on such a fine, mellow, late September afternoon that Lord Peake entertained us at tea; and, on setting out, I almost grudged having to spend the time indoors. I had expected to be entertained in a house; but Lord Peake's London establishment was a flat in a building next door to the Ritz. However, it was a spacious flat, with a view into the gardens of Buckingham Palace. "You see, I have the same view as the King," Lord Peake said, with his sly, mischievous smile, gesturing in the direction of the window; and later he

34

took us up to a roof garden, where he pointed out to us the landmarks of the city. "You can see as much from here as from St. Paul's," he said complacently. Perhaps he was right. London had no really high buildings then, except for the University of London Senate Building; but I have always been nervous of heights, and this view was quite high enough for me.

"But the sky here always looks low," I said to Paddy Newcome, who was standing next to me. "You could almost touch it."

"Nearer my God to thee," Paddy said, laughing nervously. He too was afraid of heights. And then, "What about Christ and the Devil on the pinnacle of the temple, or was it on top of the mountain? 'All these things will I give thee...'?"

We went back to Lord Peake's drawing-room, where Lord Peake's granddaugher, Lady Jemima Hunt, offered us tea and cakes. Lady Jemima was the daughter of an English earl who had married Lord Peake's daughter but was now divorced from her. She was accompanied by a young naval officer to whom she seemed to be on the verge of becoming engaged. These young persons, I suppose, had been invited in order to make us feel at home; but in fact the two sets of young people observed each other warily, as visitors to a zoo might observe the wild creatures behind the wire mesh. Goodness knows which of us were the wild creatures and which were the visitors. Perhaps we were all on display, Lord Peake himself being the most splendid lion of all.

"No tea for me, Jemmy," Lord Peake said. "I'll have something stronger. What about you, Lorna, my girl? Can I offer you something?"

"I've never drunk anything stronger than beer," I said, "and I don't like that."

"Oh, those New Brunswick women," he said, "the same as they always were. I have just the thing for someone who isn't used to drinking. A very nice Rhine wine. You'll like it, I guarantee."

35

I did like it, though I drank it suspiciously, afraid of becoming drunk and making a fool of myself.

Lord Peake exerted himself to charm, and in fact succeeded. He talked of politics, as one who had inside experience of political life; he amused us with accounts of Hyde Park orators; he told us anecdotes of a famous dramatist, lately dead, who had been his friend, and a famous novelist, still alive, who was his enemy. He inquired how we were settling down, and asked us if there were some small favour he could do us, someone we wanted to be introduced to, for example. We must visit the House of Commons. Should he get cards for us? "But anybody can get into the House of Commons," I said. "We don't need cards, do we?"

"But we might get a better place, Lorna," Chrissie said, frowning at me warningly.

"Miss Ridley wants to be independent," Lord Peake said. "Very admirable, I'm sure. Perhaps if something special comes up you may change your mind, though."

"I'll let you know," I said. I must, after all, have been slightly affected by the wine.

Evening was drawing in by the time we left. Chrissie and I wandered out into the streets of the unfamiliar city. "Let's find a place where we can get something solid to eat instead of party junk," Chrissie said; and we were soon settled in the corner of a little cafeteria eating fish and chips.

"Well, isn't this a contrast?" Chrissie exclaimed. "Half an hour ago we were in the midst of all that wealth and luxury, and now here we are." And she waved a hand in the general direction of our grubby surroundings.

"Good fish and chips, though," I said. "And nobody inspecting us."

"Really, Lorna," Chrissie said. "You could have been more polite to the Old Boy. After all, you're taking his scholarship. You might as well accept another small favour that won't cost him anything. Obviously he enjoys making these gestures. Some independence is ungenerous."

"I know, Chrissie. I have no tact. Mother tells me so all the time. But he does show off. I don't like to be patronized. And I earned the scholarship."

"Self-made, Lorna? You and Lord Peake, you're both alike. Well, never mind. What do you think of Lady Jemima? Isn't she a beautiful girl?"

"Yes," I said grudgingly. "She is beautiful. But I'd be closer to being beautiful myself if I had as much money to spend on clothes and hair and complexion as she does."

"But she doesn't look artificial, Lorna. Her complexion and hair and clothes are real."

"So much the more expensive they are, then. Like good, simple clothes. Anything real costs a lot."

"Well, you and I are getting a costly education. Thanks to Lord Peake. But isn't it remarkable how a rough, gritty product like Lord Peake—a New Brunswick small-town boy, who is still really a small-town boy—could produce something so delicate and fine and flower-like as Lady Jemima? Doesn't that show that education and environment are more important than heredity?"

"I don't know about that. She's only a Peake on her mother's side. Perhaps the ladies of the Hunt family have always been fine and flower-like. And maybe she'll be gritty 30 or 40 years from now, too. Who knows?"

"Well, never mind. Perhaps she and her young man are talking over those strange Canadians. Including her grandfather."

Lord Peake continued to do his social duty by us from time to time. Was he trying to buy our gratitude, as I thought then, or was genuine kindness involved? Some homesickness, perhaps, for Canadian voices? People are not simple, and perhaps Lord Peake himself could not have altogether explained his own motives.

I remember a luncheon, at which the Vice-Chancellor of the University of London—a woman—was present; and an evening party that lasted until the early hours of the next morning. The warden of the university hostel where I was staying was angry with me because I had not got special permission and the front door key in advance. I had to ring the emergency door bell, and she herself came down in curlers and a dressing-gown and scolded me because she thought I might have come to some bad end on the streets. She would hardly believe that I had been at a party at Lord Peake's; and even when she did believe it, seemed to suspect that Lord Peake was a corrupter of youth.

Was it at that party that I angered Lord Peake by telling him that I never read the *Clarion*? No—I read *The Times* and the *Manchester Guardian*. I hadn't time for the *Clarion* too.

"But I don't like the *Clarion*," I said to Chrissie the next time I saw her. "It's a gossip sheet. Why should I read it?"

"You could look at it now and then, especially just before one of Lord Peake's parties. It's only common gratitude. And the paper's not that bad. It has a personality, as he does himself."

"He doesn't own my mind. I'll read what I want."

Nevertheless, grudgingly, I did read the *Clarion* now and then. And I was impressed, in spite of myself, when Lord Peake took an evening to show us over the *Clarion* offices in Fleet Street. The big, humming operation; the offices, the presses, the excitement of incoming news; the multiplicity and liveliness of the activities going on—they gave me a sense of excitement in spite of my previous determination not to find them remarkable. And at the centre of all these activities, directing them, truly at home in them, as he was not entirely at home in the other places where I had seen him, was Lord Peake. He was like a magician, attended by lesser helpers or tricky spirits, all working together to perform some miracle, or perhaps only to create an illusion. I have always admired the magician, or the illusionist, who is a kind of artist; and for a moment, maybe even for half an hour, I gave Lord Peake the credit of being such an artist. Then my critical spirit took over. I mentally accused Lord Peake of vanity instead of artistry. I deplored the finished product, the *Clarion* itself, this brash newspaper with the screaming headlines that (to my mind) contrasted so unfavourably with the sober *Times*. (*The Times* still devoted its entire front page to the classified ads and put its news stories on its discreet inner pages. Another kind of showmanship?) I criticized the *Clarion*'s style, then, as I criticized the architectural style of the *Clarion* office—vulgar, shiny, twentieth-century chrome and steel and concrete in the midst of dignified, settled structures from the Victorian age and earlier. And yet, when I think of it now—was not Lord Peake right to find his own style, to be the Bold Colonial Boy in the midst of the solid, stolid British? The *Clarion* and its offices and its owner could not very well imitate *The Times*. The magician may perform old tricks, but something about his style of performing them must be different. And a newspaper must itself be news.

"And what do you think of it all, Lorna Ridley?" Lord Peake asked. "Isn't it a tremendous plaything? Wouldn't you like to work in a place like this?"

"No." I said. "I don't think I'd care to. I still like *The Times* better."

He shook his head. His face clouded. I had spoiled his pleasure, the rather innocent pleasure of showing off his little empire to someone young and poor who came from the place where he had been young and poor.

Perhaps the climax of Lord Peake's hospitality came in late February, when he invited us all to his country place, Tantramar Hall, named for those New Brunswick marshes near which he had grown up. We were motored down in a small bus, with Mr. Collop, the man who had met us at the dock in Liverpool, acting as our guide. It was not a long drive, at least from a North American standpoint. We arrived well before lunch. Yet we seemed clear away from London, in a world of country lanes and hedgerows, already beginning to be springlike. Tantramar Hall was on the edge of a village, but separated from it by a width of park. Clearly Lord Peake —or perhaps the late Lady Peake—had wanted the traditional home of English gentry. Yet the house, when we reached it, although large and imposing, was disappointing. It was not a genuine Stately Home of England, dating from medieval or Tudor times, or even from the eighteenth century. Neither was it brashly and cheekily modern, like the office of the *Clarion*. It was a solid, sturdy late Victorian house that had been made as convenient as a late Victorian house could be made. The furniture of the lounge where Lord Peake greeted us was comfortable and undistinguished. The paintings on the walls were good paintings by living English painters, but, surprisingly, almost too safe. They included a painting of Lord Peake himself, perhaps twenty years younger, a short, square, vital man, painted larger than life, and one (I think Mr. Collop told us later) of Lord Peake's late wife, a pale, pretty, rather dispirited woman.

Lady Jemima was not present this time; but her mother, who was plain Mrs. Arnold (having remarried after divorcing Lady Jem's father) helped Lord Peake entertain us. She was a pleasant, rather faded middle-aged woman who slightly resembled her mother's portrait.

"Are you very chilly after that bus trip?" she inquired anxiously.

"No," Chrissie said, "but what a beautiful fire."

A lively blaze was crackling away in the fireplace, and I found a seat near it.

"I know Canadians always like warm rooms," Mrs. Arnold said. "Father does."

"These young Canadians have probably been spending a very cold winter," Lord Peake said. "The combination of English weather and English heating, or lack of it, is the very devil. I've never got used to it." He himself had just come back from a month in a warmer climate, and looked brown-skinned and healthy.

After our preliminary drinks, we were taken to the dining-room for lunch. To my dismay, I found myself placed next to Lord Peake, with Chrissie opposite me. I hoped he would make speeches to the table in general rather than talk to me; and so he did for some of the time, mentioning in passing the opening of Parliament, which was to take place the first of March. Eventually, however, he turned to me.

"Well, Lorna Ridley," he said, "I think you are the only one here who hasn't asked me for a small favour—an introduction, a visit to some institution. Have you thought yet of something you would like?"

"Yes," I said. "You told us you could get us cards for a special occasion at the House of Commons. What about that opening of Parliament, with the Speech from the Throne?"

"The opening of Parliament, when both Lords and Commons meet? I'm afraid you've asked for the one day when I can't get you in as a visitor. Nobody can get you in for that day. Pick any other day of the Session, Lorna. Or pick some other favour."

"Oh, but that's the one day I want," I said. "If it isn't difficult it isn't a favour, is it? I'm not interested in Parliament; but I'd like to be there and hear the King give his speech."

"I'm sorry, Lorna. It can't be done. There's only one way you can get in."

"What's that?" I asked.

"You can find a handsome young peer and marry him. Or become a peeress in your own right. Peeresses are the only women visitors who can be present for the Throne Speech."

41

He twinkled at the table in general. He had turned a defeat into a victory, and was teasing me.

"I wouldn't care to marry a peer," I said coldly. "It wouldn't be suitable for a Canadian."

"Is that so, Miss Ridley?" he said with equal frostiness. "Well, in that case I'm afraid you'll just have to visit Parliament some other day."

I could hardly, I realized, have done more to annoy him. I had discovered a favour that he could not manage to perform; and at the same time I had spoken rudely of the possession of a peerage to a peer—and a peer who might have had his own doubts as to the value of peerages. (Would he have been better off without that peerage? Had it cut him off from the genuine power he had wanted?)

The rest of the visit passed well enough. Nevertheless, shortly afterwards, when the time for renewal of scholarships came, I was not astonished that mine was not renewed. Professor Hamish, my adviser at King's, was puzzled, however. "I don't understand," he said. "I recommended you highly. I was sure you would be here another year."

"Oh," I said, "I imagine it's just that Lord Peake didn't like me."

"Perhaps you're right," he said. "He sounds like a strange man."

Not so very strange, I thought. It was only what I might have expected of Lord Peake. Still, I was half disappointed. He ought to have been more generous. After all, he himself had told me to speak up. But it was something to have been able to make him angry. Anger was not indifference. An indifferent man would have allowed the scholarship to be renewed, if only to prove that he was not unjust.

"Never mind," Professor Hamish said. "North America is the place to be now, isn't it? If I were young, I'd go there myself."

"Would you really?" I asked.

"Yes. Toronto or California or one of those places."

He sounded as if they were in each other's backyards, like Oxford or Cambridge.

For a long time I was angry with Lord Peake. I thought I might have been at home in England, and he had prevented me from being at home there. Now—how do I know that it wasn't a favour to send me back to Canada? Chrissie stayed in London for five years, and then moved to New York. The last time I saw her, she told me she didn't feel at home anywhere. Was Lord Peake at home anywhere? Well, yes, he was at home in the *Clarion* offices.

One of Lord Peake's biographers says that he saw himself as a failure, that he never had the political power he was capable of holding, that the ideas he had given his life to (unity of the Commonwealth, for example) were outmoded. Perhaps he thought the only success he had with those scholarship winners was the cut in his taxes. Well, in absolute terms, of course, everyone's a failure. If he wanted absolute power, absolute influence, undying devotion, he could not possibly succeed. I've laughed at him, heaven knows, like everybody else, when he expected gratitude for all those benefactions named after himself. Nevertheless, now that he is safely dead, now that he can't come back and haunt me (or can he?) I have to admit that he had a kind of success as far as I was concerned. Did I hate the old bastard, or did I love him?

Yes, Jeremy Peake, out there in whatever space you now inhabit. I'm not giving up. I'm trying to speak out. But with my own voice, I tell you, in my own style.

the letters

Old Mrs. Carfax, Muriel Melton's mother, was, Muriel had realized, suffering her final illness, though she was not quite sure whether her mother knew it. Muriel and Jake, her husband, had fixed up a downstairs room for Mrs. Carfax, so that Muriel would not have to be running upstairs all day to look after her mother. It was a large room, with as many of Mrs. Carfax's belongings from her old home as could be crammed into it: her big bed, of course; the bedside table with its Bible and medicine; a sofa on which Muriel sometimes spent part of the night, if she was worried about her mother; a stiff-backed

Victorian chair covered with tapestry; a rocking-chair; a little cupboard with a few odds and ends of glass dishes and trinkets and some family photographs (Muriel and Jake; Pauline and her family; Mrs. Carfax's husband); a desk with pigeonholes for letters; the vanity-table with mirror that had reflected Ada Carfax when she was a young married woman with her dark hair worn in a puff over her forehead and those beautiful amber eyes that young George Carfax had so much admired. She was still, Muriel thought, a pretty woman, even in her seventies, with her curling white hair and those pink cheeks that illness had not made entirely pale.

"Well," Muriel said, "it's still keeping pretty cool in here even if it's hot outside."

She came in carrying a tray with two glasses of lemonade and some of the ginger cookies she had been baking. It was the middle of the morning on a hot July day, time for a break. Also time for her mother's pills.

She was relieved that her mother was better today than on some days. The day before, she had been wandering in her mind (the pills? senility? probably both) and had got Muriel mixed up with her own mother. Strange children, she had said, were walking through the walls and jumping on her bed. She had wanted Muriel to protect her from them. Almost every day she told Muriel, "Your father came to see me last night. He was looking well." As if George Carfax had not been in his grave for nearly two years. And sometimes she said, "Pauline was here, but she wouldn't stay. Pauline will never stay."

Pauline ought to come and help look after Mother for a few days, Muriel thought. But, she reminded herself, Pauline, her sister, who was fourteen years younger than she was, had children at home to look after, and Tom, her husband, was a shiftless man, not one to take hold and look after the farm and the family if Pauline went away for a while.

Today Mrs. Carfax did not mention any visitors and

45

seemed as lucid as before her illness. She took the glass of lemonade from Muriel and said, smiling, "Thank you, dear. You're a good daughter. I don't know what I'd do without you." And Muriel, who had always adored her mother (for her strength, her courage, her truthfulness, and the beauty of her eyes) felt blessed and grateful, and for the time being not jealous of Pauline, who had seemed to her in the past to be her mother's favourite.

Mrs. Carfax, sipping her lemonade and making a face over her pill, said, "Muriel, I've been thinking I should go over some of those old packets of letters in the desk there and tear them up. Throw them away. If something should happen to me, I wouldn't want you to have the trouble."

So she does know, Muriel thought. I wouldn't have minded reading some of those old letters. Oh well.

"You might enjoy going over them," she said to her mother. "Living over your life, sort of."

"Not quite. The most important things aren't on paper, I suppose. I've never been one to look behind, most of my life. But lying here like this does make it all come back, sometimes. Anyhow, down in that bottom pigeonhole, to the right, there's a bundle of your father's letters to me. Do you think you could get them out?"

It was a fat bundle. Two bundles. Her father's letters, in a handwriting that was familiar to Muriel, but yet slightly different, smoother and rounder somehow. Younger, of course, she realized. The paper yellowing. "Love letters," her mother sighed. "Your father's love letters. He didn't keep mine to him. But he said he could remember them all anyway."

Muriel went back to the kitchen, leaving her mother lying back on her pillows with one of the bundles of letters in her hands.

When she returned, her mother was tearing up one of the letters, a look of regret on her face. She put on a cheerful expression for Muriel, however. "These aren't the first of your father's letters to be torn up, Muriel," she said. "Did I ever tell you that story?"

"No, Mother. Were you mad at Papa then?"

"No. I wasn't the one who tore the letter up. Did you ever hear of Ethan Ward?"

"No, I don't think so. I don't remember the name. Who was he?"

"He was someone I went around with back at the Cape before your father came there to teach. The Wards lived next door to us. Ethan and I went to school together. I guess he thought he was my best beau and I would marry him. But I never took him as seriously as he took me."

"So he and Papa were rivals, then?"

"Oh, he wasn't your father's rival. He didn't count at all, as soon as I saw George. But he thought they were rivals. Well, George and I went steady all that year he taught at the Cape, and the next year, when George moved to Charlestown to teach, we agreed to be married in another year. He would save his money, and I would sew tablecloths for my hope chest, the way girls did then, and the next summer we would be married."

"I remember Papa talking about that part. But how does Ethan Ward fit in?"

"Well, when George went away, I guess Ethan thought it was just a matter of time before I'd forget about George and go with him again. Of course I didn't, and he was disappointed. But one day I had just come out of the house with a letter in my hand for your father, intending to mail it at the post office, when Ethan came out too. 'Why Ada,' he said to me, 'let me take your letter, and I'll mail it and save you a trip.' I don't know why I didn't just say I'd like the walk; but I guess maybe I thought then he would ask to walk with me,

47

and I didn't want his company. So I gave him the letter."

"Did you think he might tear it up?"

"No, I didn't think he'd be so silly. But I guess what he thought was that if George didn't get a letter from me he'd be mad, and wouldn't write. Then of course I wouldn't write again either, and Ethan would have me on the rebound."

"But how did you find out?"

"Well, your father and I figured it out between us. Of course Ethan's plan didn't work because we didn't wait for answers to our letters. We wrote to each other twice a week, or at least once a week. But we knew there was a letter missing; I had given George some news in that letter, and I could tell from his answer that he hadn't got it. A month or so later, Ethan saw me out with a letter again, and he looked at me with a queer look. 'I'm mailing this one myself, Ethan,' I said, and you know, he never spoke to me again. He left town shortly after and moved West to work, and I guess his family almost never heard from him. Ethan wasn't a letter writer himself."

"I'm glad his plan didn't work, anyway. I wouldn't have wanted Ethan Ward as a father. He sounds sneaky to me."

"Oh I don't know. I wasn't so much mad as amused. After all, he didn't do any harm. And he must've thought a lot of me in his way."

The ghost of that pretty girl, Ada Glenn, who had married young George Carfax, seemed almost tangible in the room. Forgiving Ethan Ward because he had been in love with her. Muriel, a dumpy middle-aged woman, felt for a moment older than her mother. Jake was the only man she had ever been out with, and they had been married a long time. A sensible marriage. They liked each other.

Jake came home at noon from the stove foundry where he worked. They lived close enough that he might as well come home for a hot meal rather than taking sandwiches. He was a

48

big, good-humoured, gentle man, not much of a talker. Lucky, Muriel thought, that he and her mother liked one another. Her mother always said, "Jake's my favourite son-in-law." And so she should. Pauline's Tom was no prize.

He stood in the door of the bedroom for a few minutes after lunch and said, "How's it going today, Old Girl? Did the mailman bring you letters? Something from Pauline?"

"Old letters, Jake. My mailman came a long time ago."

"Well, keep up your spirits. Any little thing you'd like?"

"No, Jake, nothing. Who's that man behind you?"

"Nobody. There's nobody here but Muriel and me."

At the back door, on his way out to work, he stopped and shook his head at Muriel. "The old girl's slipping," he said. "When they begin to see visitors as she does, they're not long for this world."

"It's not fair," Muriel answered. "Why does she have to go like that? She was so good this morning, too, just like her old self."

When Muriel went back into the bedroom, her mother was sitting bolt upright in the bed, staring at a spot directly in front of her. "Tell him to go away, Muriel," she said. "Tell him I don't like him. It's that Ethan Ward come to see me again."

"Oh, Mother, it's because you were talking about him this morning. Ethan Ward's not here."

"Yes, he is here too. He's here and he's laughing at me. He says I have no right to criticize him because I'm just like him."

"Mother, how can you be like Ethan Ward? But he can't hurt you. Nobody can hurt you while I'm here. Look, it's time for your lunch. Jake and I had ours. Why don't I bring you a nice chicken sandwich and a cup of tea?"

"I'm not hungry."

"See how you feel when I bring it."

Mrs. Carfax only picked at the sandwich when Muriel brought it, but she did drink the tea, and it seemed to clear her head. "He's gone now," she said. "I hope he doesn't come back."

"What did you mean, Mother," Muriel asked, "saying you were like him?"

Mrs. Carfax turned the teacup around on her saucer. "Maybe I should tell you, Muriel," she said. "I might feel better if I told someone. Only don't tell Pauline."

"What has it got to do with Pauline?"

Mrs. Carfax was silent for a time. "Do you remember," she asked finally, "when Pauline was going with Connor Gregory?"

"Yes. Of course I was already married and not around the house much, but I knew she was going with him. I didn't think much of him, though he might have been better than Tom."

She conjured up a mental picture of Connor Gregory, tall, red-haired, lively. A little too much given to drink. A divorced man, in a day when divorce was less common than now. Not the sort of man she liked seeing her little sister go with. But Pauline had a will of her own. Her mother's amber eyes.

"I didn't think much of him either. But there was no arguing with Pauline if she wanted anyone or anything. She was a little like me that way. But Connor Gregory and your father weren't the same man. Anyhow, I hoped they'd break up before any harm was done. They'd have a fight, maybe, or see someone else, or just get bored."

"How did it end, finally? That was around the time I was going to have the baby and lost it, and I don't think I was noticing other people much. Connor went away, didn't he?"

"Yes, he went away, all the way to British Columbia to work. He wasn't a letter writer like your father, either.

Pauline used to come home from school—she was in her last year of high school—and she would look for a letter from him. She was almost always disappointed."

"Well, I suppose it just petered out, then, and he found someone else, and she married Tom."

"It wasn't quite like that. A letter did come, finally. I was alone in the house, and I don't know what took hold of me, but I steamed it open. I thought I would just see what was in it and then seal it up again and give it to Pauline."

Muriel was startled. Her mother, who had always taught them never to look even at a letter that had already been opened if it belonged to someone else. However, she tried to cover her surprise. "Was there anything special in the letter?" she asked.

"Yes, he wanted her to go out to Vancouver right away. He said he had a home for them. He said if she agreed to this to write right back and he would send her the fare for a ticket by the next mail. Well, I was very upset by this. I thought no good would come of it—my little girl going all the way to Vancouver by herself before she was even married. I thought that if he had really cared for her he would have come back to get her. At first I sealed up the letter and thought I would give it to her, and then argue with her. But how did I know she would tell me what he had asked her to do? Pauline always kept her thoughts to herself. So finally I tore it up, and I didn't tell her about it."

"What happened then? Didn't Pauline suspect something? Didn't he write to her again, or didn't she write to him?"

"No. He wasn't like your father. He didn't write again. If he had I'd have given her the letter, I'd decided that. But there were no more letters and I suppose she was too proud to write to him. Almost immediately she started going out with Tom, and married him that summer. I realized why when the baby was born early. All these years I've never dared tell her for fear she'd say I'd ruined her life."

Muriel was stunned by these revelations. Would Pauline say that? Had her life been ruined? There was no knowing now. She tried to comfort her mother: "Well, Tom's not so bad," she said. "He's not the world's greatest provider and he drinks even more than Connor Gregory did, but they jog along well enough most of the time. They have a nice family." And she thought with a pang of Pauline's children. She had sometimes envied Pauline for having them, though goodness knows they were a handful. Did Pauline sometimes envy her her own snug, childless life with good, sensible, hard-working Jake?

"Do you really think she's happy, Muriel?" Mrs. Carfax said wistfully. "Do you think I ought to tell her? Has she felt betrayed all these years because she thinks Connor didn't want her? Would she forgive me for not telling her?"

"I hardly know what to say," Muriel answered in bewilderment. Then, after a little thought, "No, I don't think I'd tell her. What good would it do now? She's contented enough with her life. Connor's probably been married for years to someone else. She might as well blame Connor as blame you."

"I suppose you're right, Muriel," Mrs. Carfax said, sighing. "Sometimes I've wondered if she did guess. She never does things for me the way you do."

"Oh, you know Pauline's fond of you. She's always so busy, that's all. Boy, I'd better get a wiggle on myself, and start thinking of something for supper. I think I'll make a potato salad. It's too warm out there this afternoon for hot food. Anything you want now?"

"I'm all right, Muriel. You go along. You're a good girl. If it were you, I know you wouldn't hold it against me."

Was that true? Just as well she couldn't know if it were true, perhaps.

Slicing the extra potatoes she had cooked at noon, chopping up celery and onion, she thought, "I'm glad I wasn't Mother's favourite." And then, "I'm glad Jake always lived nearby and didn't write letters."

As she mixed in the oil and vinegar, her mind continued working. Had she been right to persuade her mother not to tell Pauline? Yes, she knew she had been right. Let sleeping dogs lie. As her grandmother used to say. Anyhow the best argument was the one she had forgotten to use. The best argument was that story her mother had told her about Ethan Ward and her mother's letter. After all, as her mother had said, Ethan hadn't done any harm; so her mother couldn't have done any harm either. It was Connor's fault and Pauline's fault, for not writing again.

Two weeks later, at her mother's funeral, Muriel stood beside Pauline in the mourners' pew. Jake and Tom were both pall-bearers, suited and correct. (Thank goodness, Tom had stayed sober.) Why was it, she wondered, that Pauline was crying so much harder than she was? After all, she knew she would miss her mother more than Pauline would, even though just at the moment her chief emotion was relief. Watching by the bed-side the last week or so had been hard. Please God I don't go that way, she prayed. They were playing one of her mother's favourite hymns now, "The King of Love my Shepherd is." Who was the King of Love? God, or George Carfax? Or John Glenn, Ada Glenn's father, the old farmer and lumberjack, carrying his little girl home? At the end she had thought she was a child.

Perverse and foolish, oft I strayed
but yet in love he sought me....

Oh, she was going to cry now, though she had thought she couldn't. Why shouldn't her mother be perverse and foolish, like everybody else? Nearly everybody else?

53

And on his shoulder gently laid,
and home returning brought me.

Well, she hoped, for her mother's sake, it was all true. Maybe
it was.

She thought, with almost a gleam of pleasure, "I share a
secret with her now. A secret Pauline doesn't know." The secret
was a weight, a responsibility. Yet, since by keeping it she
could do a favour to both her mother and Pauline, protect
them both, it was also a privilege.

She looked at Pauline's face, all blubbered with crying, and
reached out and squeezed her arm. The two women stood
with hands clasped watching as their men, with the other
pallbearers, lifted the coffin and carried their mother up the
aisle and out of the church to the waiting hearse.

a nest of dolls

"Clemmy wants us to go to her place for dinner Thursday night, Anna," Edith says. "Thursday because it's her day off. And it's just after pay day."

Clemmy is Clementina, Edith's daughter, my niece. Edith and I are sitting in Edith's tiny apartment drinking tea: strong, bitter New Brunswick tea, not weak English slop, as Edith might have put it. Edith is in her sixties, though she still has an air of youth. She is smoking a cigarette, which I look at with the mild distaste of the non-smoker— resignedly, however, because there is no arguing with Edith.

I'm the younger of the two, the career woman (as Edith sometimes describes me) visiting on summer vacation.

I have mixed feelings about visiting my relatives, very mixed. On this visit, my annual visit, I stay at a neighbouring hotel, as usual, so as to be able to withdraw some of the time, to be independent. But I have lunch fairly regularly with Edith. I've given Edith some extra money, so as not to be a burden. (There are always ghosts whispering in my ear, "Don't be beholden to anyone. Always pay your own way." Ghosts from far back in time, my Depression childhood. People don't say "beholden" any longer.) Nevertheless, I feel guilty toward Edith because my apartment is so much bigger than hers; my salary is so much more than her pension. How can she ever forgive me? Perhaps she doesn't. Though of course it isn't my fault, is it? One doesn't fail in order to be one of the family.

"How are Clemmy and her family?" I ask dutifully.

It's a long story. It always is. Clemmy, like Edith herself, has lived a varied life. Her early, teenage marriage to an untalented country-and-western musician who drifted off aimlessly into the unknown, ended in divorce; she has lived with several men, finally marrying a Good Worker who, however, beat her up and nearly killed her before she left him. Now she has a job in a supermarket. The children of her first marriage had already left home before the second marriage broke up; but there are two teenagers, Dylan and Dilys, children of a lover who preceded the Good Worker. I don't know why both Edith and Clemmy run to such fancy names for their children. If I had a daughter, I'd name her Jane or Mary Ellen. Edith has a Blodwen, too, the elder daughter, who's religious and has joined the Pentecostals. Edith can't stand Blodwen, and never takes me to visit her, though she lives near Clemmy, just across the street in fact.

"Dylan's great on sport but not on school," Edith tells me.

"But Dilys is a dandy little student. Just like you were. She's won a prize for a short story. Second prize, but a prize."

I try to recall Dilys' age. I have so many nieces, nephews, grandnieces. One of my brothers has ten kids. No kidding, as you might say. Dilys, Edith tells me, will be thirteen next month. I remember myself at thirteen, a thin, shy little creature, dodging the kisses of all those aunts, uncles and cousins. (My mother was one of twelve.) Writing sermons in my scribbler. Sermons, no less. I must buy some little present for Dilys, I think.

"What time does Clemmy want us there?" I ask.

"What time? What time?" Edith echoes. "We're visiting family, not one of your fancy friends who has the meal set for a particular time. We'll go in the afternoon so we'll have lots of time to yak. The bus goes only once an hour. We can take it over there around 3.30."

That early? I think. Will we have enough to say to last us however long it will be before we can decently leave? Again I feel guilty. My fault also that I don't expect us to have anything to say to one another?

That afternoon I visit the shopping-mall and buy the nest of dolls for Dilys. Or maybe for myself.

It's the middle of June, but cool and rather damp. Thursday afternoon is not rainy, but looks as if it might rain at any moment. Edith frowns at me because I carry an umbrella. She disapproves of my caution as much as I disapprove of her smoking. But we are stuck with one another. In fact, we need one another, though we couldn't bear to live in the same space, or perhaps even in the same town.

The bus crosses the river, seems to ramble deviously around streets for a long time before Edith says it's time to get off. Clemmy lives not far from a bus-stop, downstairs in a house. There are other tenants upstairs. We pass children and dogs on the way to the front door. Clemmy has seen us coming, and opens the door before Edith can ring the bell. She must be in her late thirties by now, but looks younger; a genuine blonde to begin with, though by now her hair must be going grey under the added colour. (Our family goes grey early, and Edith and I have both given up by this time trying to repair those particular ravages of time.) Her cheeks are pink, her forehead still smooth, her eyes blue. She is short, plumpish, curving in all the right places. The sort of woman who makes lovers and husbands jealous, so that they beat her up and treat her badly.

"Come in, Aunt Anna," she says. "You're quite a stranger. How long are you here for? Let me take your umbrella."

The little living-room is comfortably enough furnished, rather like a room in a mail-order catalogue. The most conspicuous object is the large colour TV, which seems to occupy half the room. Opposite the TV, on a sofa, Dilys is sitting. She is slight, with long, fair hair, wearing blue jeans and a yellow shirt. She looks a bit like her mother, but is more serious, less bouncy. She gets up to take the parcel I hand her, thanks me with smiling composure, like a little lady. She is not shy, as I was at her age; neither is she brash. I wish fleetingly that she were not so pretty. Perhaps I envy her; I'd prefer to think I would like her to be plain for the time being merely so that she would have fewer distractions getting through school. It would be a pity, I think, for her to contract a young, disastrous marriage, like her mother and her grandmother before her.

Delicious smells waft in from the kitchen. Clemmy is roasting a turkey, doing very well by her visiting aunty. A good cook, Clemmy. Not a bad housekeeper, either. A good mother, daughter, sister. In fact, except for her unfortunate taste in husbands and lovers, Clemmy is a model young (young-ish?) woman.

Edith and I share the sofa with Dilys. Edith pats the arm of the sofa and tells me, "It's new. Clemmy bought it with her

58

income tax return. Paid cash for it."

"Aren't you opening your parcel, Dilys?" Clemmy asks.

Dilys unwraps the parcel carefully, folding the paper, smoothing out the ribbon, taking care not to damage the bow. It's one of those Russian dolls, made of wood, which unscrews and reveals, as if in a nest, another doll, inside which is still another, so that eventually there are five or six dolls, the last one being of the most absurd tininess. A toy, and yet a grown-up toy. I would like to have one myself. Dilys is pleased. She touches each of the dolls wonderingly with her finger. "They're all hand painted," she says. She gets up from the sofa and lines up the group of dolls on the floor in front of the television, as if they were watching it. Her mother takes her place on the sofa, and we all turn our attention to the picture.

It's a soap opera, with people engaged in plots and counterplots. I'm not sure what is going on, but recognize that there is one totally good woman and a couple of villainesses. There is adultery, drug smuggling and a threatened murder. I glance at Dilys. My mother, I think, would not have liked me to see a film like that when I was thirteen. I didn't see a movie until I was fourteen, and then it was one of the Tarzan movies. Edith, I think, guesses what's in my mind. Or perhaps she's thinking the same thing. "It's not a bad show," she says defensively. "After all, life's like that."

"Is it?" I ask. "Maybe life imitates TV."

My life isn't like that. I've never met a villain, I think. Some of my friends' children have been up on drug charges, but they don't belong to any mafia, goodness knows. Merely your average stupid young persons. No special glamour. The middle-aged adulterers I know aren't villainous either. Or glamorous, for that matter.

Well, it's a trashy show, but I don't suppose it will harm Dilys. At her age I read all the time. Some good stuff, some abominable stuff. *Gone With the Wind,* for heaven's sake. There

59

was a piece of high-class trash for you.

Clemmy gets up to look at the turkey, and I follow her into the kitchen. We sit at the kitchen-table talking, while the television chatters on in the other room. She tells me again about the last days of her second marriage: how James, her husband, got drunk and tried to strangle her, and Dylan managed to pull him off while Edith, who was visiting, ran for help. "Sound like a soap opera?" she asks, laughing, though rather grimly.

"Yes," I say. Then, "No. Not entirely. James wasn't handsome enough for TV."

"Radio," she says. "Oxydol's own Ma Perkins. He could have been on it."

We eat in the kitchen: Edith, Clemmy and I, that is. Dilys and Dylan (who comes in late) take their plates and eat in the living-room. I don't know what they are watching now. Early news? Earthquakes, tidal waves, natural disasters? Wars or politics or hostage taking? It would give me indigestion to eat dinner during the news.

Eating is a serious matter. We don't interrupt it by much conversation. Just "Pass the pickles," maybe. Something like that. Edith says it's just like Christmas, all that turkey and stuffing. Dessert is strawberry shortcake: real shortcake, not cake, not ordinary biscuits. Her grandmother's recipe, bless her. Edith and I "Oh" and "Ah" nostalgically. The whipped cream is real, too, not that stuff out of a can. A perfect niece, Clemmy.

While we are drinking tea, Blodwen, Edith's other daughter, and her daughter Beulah come in. Blodwen is dark, nervous, with a throaty voice. Beulah is the same age as Dilys, but fat. She eats shortcake, a blob of whipped cream on her nose. Dilys shows her the dolls. "They're all hand-painted," she repeats; and shows her how they fit into one another. The two cousins stand side by side, like two of the dolls, inspecting them.

I should, I think, buy a similar nest of dolls for Beulah. That would be only fair. But then, why should I be fair? Life isn't fair. Some girls are prettier than others, smarter, win more prizes. Not all girls have parents who love them. People have to get used to unfairness of that kind.

Why doesn't Edith love Blodwen as much as she loves Clemmy, for instance? (Edith knows I wonder about this. Sometimes she has said to me angrily, "Because she isn't lovable, that's why. I can't make myself love her, can I?" No, of course not. No reason why mothers should be compelled to love daughters. Or why one should love sisters or cousins or aunts or nieces. Love's never an obligation, is it? Whatever the Bible says. The Bible, which Blodwen will quote at the drop of a hat, if she gets a chance.)

Now Edith is coolly polite to Blodwen as if she were an acquaintance she had met half a dozen times; while Blodwen is solicitous of her mother, trying to persuade her to stop smoking. (She used to smoke herself, of course, before her conversion.) She tries too hard, I think. Her husky voice is too urgent. She makes large, enveloping gestures, as if she would love us all if she were allowed. But she doesn't stay long. She and Bruce, her husband, are off to a prayer meeting. She has just called in to say hello, she says.

The telephone rings. Dylan, the young man of sixteen, answers it, goes off, he says, with the boys. Edith, Clemmy and I settle in the living-room again with refilled cups. The television is still going. Dilys is sitting on the floor in front of it, doing her homework. She glances at it now and then abstractedly, while her pencil runs on. Edith and Clemmy shout at each other amicably over the sound of the canned voices, exchanging bits of news. I sit and watch Dilys, imagine transporting her to her own large, quiet room in my apartment, with no TV, no distraction. She would probably loathe it. She isn't my imaginary daughter, my Mary Ellen, who would fit so tidily into my life.

I try to see the world through her eyes, what it must have been like to lose her own father, be moved in on by a cruel stepfather. (But James wasn't cruel to Dilys; it was Dylan he couldn't get on with—not to mention Clemmy, of course.) If she writes a journal, what will she say in it about today?

Tonight Gramma and Mum's Aunt Anna came to supper.
Mum cooked a turkey and a strawberry shortcake. (Yum!)
Aunt Anna gave me the cutest set of dolls, which all fit inside one another. Aunt Anna is...

No, it's what she remembers 40 years from now that will be interesting. If she remembers anything. Aunt Anna's visit and the dolls, a quiet evening in front of the old-fashioned television, in contrast with whatever horrors or luxuries emerge in that future time. She will be travelling in space, perhaps, and remember tonight, see herself as she is now, enclosed in the self that will exist then.

They are showing a program now appealing for money for the poor children of the world. There are scrawny, under-nourished children, diseased children, children on crutches and in rags. Dilys puts down her pencil, watches the set with undivided attention, her chin in her hand. What is she think-ing? Does she also suffer guilt because she has, for the moment, more than others: her good dinner, her jeans, her dolls, her mother, the TV, her long fair hair and pink cheeks and straight limbs? Her prize, even though it was only a second prize? Is she meditating on some act of self-sacrifice, of dedication, when she is grown up? When I was her age, writing those sermons in my scribbler, I wanted to be a missionary. Not now, though. The injustice, the absurdity of the world is too huge for me to fight, except in a small way.

Anyhow, I refuse to feel guilty because I have just had a good dinner. I too have been hungry in my time, may be again, for all I know.

"Awful, isn't it?" Clemmy says.

"Yes," Edith agrees, "but there's poor people right here in Canada too. Look after your own first, I always say. Some folks would give money to missionaries and foreigners that wouldn't help their own flesh and blood."

Is she afraid of starving herself, I wonder? Might I— Clemmy—Dilys send money away that could help her in her old age? No, I'm being unjust. It's only something to say, one of Edith's letters to the editor, which she loves to write. Or perhaps she's arguing with herself, telling herself not to be a fool and take money out of her pension to send to poor babies in India. We all feel guilty, fight off guilt, imagine guilt in others.

Edith inquires when the next bus leaves for the other side of the river. Clemmie and Dilys disagree: it might be fifteen minutes, it might be twenty.

"You won't have time to read all of it," Edith says to me, "but you should read part of Dilys' story. The one she got the prize for."

"Would you mind letting me read it?" I ask Dilys. I remember that I hid those sermons; they were for myself, not to be preached to anyone.

But Dilys doesn't have my adolescent urge for secrecy. She nods composedly, goes off to her room and brings back the story, written out on lined paper in her round, girlish hand.

The first thing I notice about it is that it's badly spelled. Well, that's not surprising. Watching TV doesn't provide lessons in spelling, the lessons that reading, even trash, provided for me. But what about the story? It's not about Dilys, anyhow. Maybe it's about Dylan. It's about a boy, a young athlete, a runner, who is running a race for a prize he covets

63

with all his heart. The boy is one of a happy family of brothers, sisters, father, mother. It's all very cosy. No battered wives or children mentioned here. They all—parents, brothers, sisters—want the boy to win the prize. There is a scene at breakfast, with lots of dialogue over the cornflakes and cheerios. But there is something wrong. The boy has angina (she spells it "anjina") and has to take pills so he won't have a heart attack. (She's picked up the word, and the pills, from Edith; it's one of Edith's ailments, one of the reasons she shouldn't be smoking.) So anyway how can the boy— Richard, his name is—win a race?

"We have to leave now," Edith tells me, "if we want to catch that bus."

I flip to the last page of the story to see how it ends. Yes, poor Richard dies. But he does win the prize. With his dying breath. Good for him. It was an impressive funeral, too, with everybody weeping, and the promise of a memorial tablet in the church.

"I didn't read all of it, but I enjoyed what I read," I tell Dilys and she nods politely, with the graciousness of a veteran receiver of compliments.

Clemmy brings my umbrella. As Edith and I back out of the front door, giving Clemmy our ritual kisses and thanks, Dilys smiles at us from her place on the floor. "Thank you, Aunt Anna, for the dolls," she says, patting the large one, which now contains the whole family. Then she picks up her pencil again, raises her eyes to the TV for guidance, and continues with the work of the evening.

64

visiting aunt alix

Something about the hotel-room where I am staying in Toronto reminds me of the times when I used to visit Aunt Alix back in the country in New Brunswick. I can't think what it is. The wallpaper maybe? The room is papered in brown, with patterns of stylized brown leaves alternating with rectangles. It creates an illusion of being a lace or tapestry, rather like that beige lace I remember seeing on somebody's windows as a child—Aunt Alix's windows? I'm not sure. In the bathroom the wallpaper is oriental: turbaned gentlemen sitting on rugs, ladies in flowing robes walking

65

under shady trees, horsemen and archers in pursuit of deer, or are they gazelles? Aunt Alix might have had a paper like that in her kitchen. I remember once, on a visit with my mother, watching the two women papering the kitchen: their anxiety that ends should match, the snipping, the glueing that went on as they shooed away children and cats, what a fine, happy mess they were in. Gay little figures of some kind there were on that wallpaper, but I can't remember what they were.

There's a print of the Peaceable Kingdom here in the hotel-room—lions, cows and tigers reposing together, with children playing near them and adults (Indians, white men) conversing happily in the distance. It hangs, slightly awry, over the desk. No paintings like that at Aunt Alix's. Not that I remember. There was Queen Victoria in her widow's cap, I think, when I first visited, but she was hung away later, somewhere in an attic.

Or is it the bed, with its large tubular bolster at the head and its white candlewick bedspread? That's it, I think. The lamp is above the bed. On the lampshade a series of camel riders—three? four? five?—are making their way across the desert sands. A chain dangles from the lamp, and when I woke last night in the middle of the night and groped around for it, confused because of the unlikeness of the room to my bedroom in Edmonton, I thought of the last time I visited Aunt Alix and reached for a similar chain above a similar bed.

But of course when I first visited Aunt Alix the chain would not have been there, because they did not have electricity. There would have been a lamp by the bed, a kerosene lamp. I see it now. A fancy lamp for the guest-room, a base with large blue flowers. Aunt Alix would have led the way into the room, carrying the lamp and setting it down on the bureau. She would have lingered for a few minutes to talk to my mother, who would be taking the pins out of her hair and letting it fall down below her waist, dark and thick. "Have you got everything you need, then, Josie?" Aunt Alix would

66

have asked. "Lots of quilts? There's more in the chest. Matches? Water for your pitcher?"

And Mother would say Yes, she knew where everything was, and then she would admire the top quilt, and maybe some others that Aunt Alix would show her. They would be sisterly together for a while, and then Aunt Alix would leave, and Mother would help me undress, and put on my flannelette nightie. I would say my prayers out loud to her— Now I lay me down to sleep—kneeling on the bed with my head in her lap: not really kneeling, because the pillowy feather tick kept pulling me down, although my mother tried to urge me to kneel. And then I would cuddle under the covers and fall deep, deep asleep in the tickly softness of it. I think Aunt Alix had the only feather beds I ever slept in.

But this could not have been my first visit. My first visit was in the daytime because we lived near enough to visit just for the day. I was so small I was only learning to walk. I seem to remember a huge, huge room with a linoleum floor—it must have been the kitchen. Aunt Alix was at one side of the room and my mother at the other, with her arms wide open, kneeling on the floor. They were urging me to walk from one side to the other. I tumbled and sat down on the shiny surface and cried. Aunt Alix pointed out the window. She said, "See the pretty flowers, Patricia. Golden glow." I tottered around, repeated "golden glow, golden glow" out loud. And then my name, as well as I could say it, "Trish, Trish."

Aunt Alix was very fat even when I first remember her. She was short—perhaps an inch or two over five feet—but she must have weighed 200 pounds. I heard my mother say this, in fact: "Your Aunt Alix weighs 200 pounds." She was in her mid-forties; her hair, I think, was already white; yet she was, in a way, still pretty. Her eyes were bright blue, her cheeks pink and fresh. She carried herself well, with an upright carriage. In fact, she rather resembled the Queen Victoria of the portrait. Because she had twice the bulk of my mother, I thought she must be twice her age; but in fact my mother was only two or three years younger.

The whole problem of age and size puzzled me greatly during those early years. "Was Aunt Alix ever young?" I asked my sister Carrie.

"Of course she was young," Carrie said. "Even Gramma was young once."

"Was Gramma young too? Were they both always fat?"

"Of course not," my mother said. "I remember your Grandma when she was young and quite thin. Alix was always plump, though, even when she was a girl, but not really fat. Pleasingly plump, that's what they used to say. Her hair was very fair, and she wore it puffed up with rats, the way everybody wore it then."

"Rats? You wore rats in your hair?" Carrie exclaimed.

"Oh, not animal rats; hair rats, headpieces, to make your hair look thicker. My own hair was so thick, I never needed to wear them. It was puffed enough by itself."

"I bet you were prettier than Aunt Alix," I said loyally.

"Some thought I was, some thought she was. People always said those Darrah girls were good lookers." She smiled, remembering.

"I always like to hear you talk about the olden days when you were young," Carrie said.

My mother laughed. It would be a long time before I understood why.

That conversation was later, several years later than the visit to the house with the golden glow. By this time I must have been five or six. We were living in another town, and sometimes, on Sunday, Uncle Dan and Aunt Alix and two or three of their children would drive over to see us. Someone—one of my cousins perhaps?—took a picture of them in the back-

68

yard: Aunt Alix and my mother with their arms around each other, Dad and Uncle Dan, Carrie and Cousin Rowena and Little Alicky. I was in the picture, too, and Teddy, the pup.

Little Alix—Alicky—was Aunt Alix's youngest, as I was my mother's, both children of our parents' middle age. Alicky was just eight months older than I was. She bossed me around, and tormented me, and sometimes treated me as a pet, and I admired and loved and hated her. Whenever we played house, she was the mother. Whenever we played school (but that was later) she played teacher. If I was the patient, she was the nurse or doctor. I somehow imagined Aunt Alix must have been like that with my mother, back when they were children, though my mother never said so.

Uncle Dan and Aunt Alix were already better off than my parents, though not so visibly so as they became later. Uncle Dan had inherited his family's farm, the Macnair farm on the Macnair Road, which was more an inheritance of poverty than of anything else; but a brother who had Gone West and made his fortune, but had never married, died and left his money to Uncle Dan. It may not have been as great a sum as the other relatives thought; but, in the days of the Depression, anybody with a little ready cash seemed wealthy. Uncle Dan could afford a new car and farm machinery; he could manage, first, to fix up the old house, then to build a new one farther up the road; he could provide his family with a piano, with a gramophone, then with a radio, the first radio I ever saw. The girls could go to Normal School or train to be nurses. Hughie, of course, would inherit the place, and it would be worth inheriting once it was running properly. Eddie wanted to wear a white collar and work in a bank.

So visiting Aunt Alix meant—at least after the very earliest years—visiting a household of solid comfort, even of some luxury. I remember the thick cream, the new-laid eggs, the butter that I watched Aunt Alix work so patiently, the heavy grey socks and mitts that she knitted for the men, her outsize silk dress for Sunday, run up on the sewing-machine, with my mother helping her. For sewing was one of my mother's skills, one of the ways in which she paid for our visits. Not to be beholden to Dan and Alix, as she would have said.

Am I to be nostalgic or am I to be truthful? For these visits, except for the very earliest ones, had their painful aspect. It's not pleasant to be poor relations, and that's what Mother and Carrie and I became; or maybe just Mother and I, since Carrie married young, and was neither poor nor rich, but struggling somewhere in the middle. My father, of course, was not a relative at all, only someone to be disapproved of for his lack of success and for not being a Good Provider for one of the Darrah girls.

I think first of one of the pleasanter visits, when Alicky and I were both ten years old. Odd that I should think it was a pleasant visit, since we had come, Mother and I, for my grandmother's funeral; but Uncle Dan's farm was so far out of town, such a distance from my grandmother's place, that I felt safe there from the scenes of Grandma's death, from her possibly angry ghost. Mother and I had come by ourselves. Dad still had his job, and Carrie, who was then fifteen, had said she would rather stay at home and cook his meals than come to the funeral. I did not miss her. Since she was becoming so grown up, she treated me, as I would have expressed it, very snottily. I enjoyed Alicky's company more. Alicky and I picked sweetpeas from the garden to put on Grandma's breast in her coffin. After the funeral Mother and I stayed for over a week at Aunt Alix's. Alicky and I rambled all over the farm talking about death and sex and our older sisters. We were still too young to menstruate, but knew about bloody periods from Carrie and Rowena. The new house with the bathroom had not yet been built, and Alicky and I took our baths in a cold brook that ran under trees, sharing a cake of green soap and splashing one another. The water came from a spring, and was almost icy, so that we came out blue and goose-pimply.

Evening

I've been downstairs to dinner in the hotel grill, a small, dark room with the menu on a blackboard. The food here is good, and I enjoyed it, even though I ate my dinner by myself, reading a novel between courses and listening to the conversation at the next table. I ate a clear consommé with a dash of sherry, a tossed salad with sour cream dressing. Arctic char. I sipped a glass of the house white wine. There was a fairly large family party at the next table, celebrating the engagement of a young couple. I took a long time over the Black Forest cake, and drank three cups of coffee. Now I am back in my room. I should phone an acquaintance or so with whom I might share a drink and a chat. And Alicky, whom I haven't seen in years, lives here. I could phone her.

But I don't feel sociable. I am still thinking of Aunt Alix. She would not have approved of wine with dinner, except maybe on Christmas Day. Neither would my mother, of course. I think of chicken soup with barley in it and home-made bread broken into it, of lettuce and tomatoes brought in from the garden, eaten with vinegar and salt; of pancakes and beans and salt pork for breakfast; of crusty strawberry short-cake with cream so thick it didn't need to be whipped. On that visit they did not grudge us the food, though sometimes, later, they did. Aunt Alix and my mother sat in the kitchen talking about my grandmother. They drew together as sisters in their grief, although both of them had had their troubles with Grandma in life.

Was it that summer that I discovered Aunt Alix's name was not really Alix? Aunt Alix, as the eldest, had inherited her mother's family Bible; and I sat in the parlour looking at the old pictures and clippings tucked within the pages; and there was the list of Grandma's children, all ten of them. But the top name, the name just before my mother's—Josephine Mary—was not Alexandra or Alix: it was Martha Henrietta. How could that be? I asked my mother in bed that night. "Well, you see, Trish, Alix didn't like her name. It was too plain for her. So once she was safely away from home and married, she just changed it. She said, 'I've decided to be Alexandra. Alix for short, like Queen Alexandra. I want you to call me that.' And we did. I never could have got away with changing my name. But Alix has a strong personality, even if she does let Dan rule the roost."

Yes, Aunt Alix had a strong personality. Alicky, though she bossed me around, was afraid of her mother. I remember once, during that visit, Aunt Alix called Alicky into her presence in the parlour. She sat in the largest chair in the room, rather as if she were sitting on a throne, and Alicky stood in front of her. I hovered apologetically in the doorway, wondering if I should stay or go out. "Well, Alicky," Auntie said majestically, "you have done quite well at school. Quite well enough. Now, I don't expect you to work at school-work in the summer. Outdoor play is good for you." (Alicky looked relieved.) "However," she continued, "I do expect you to work at your piano lessons. To practise."

"Yes, Mamma," Alicky said docilely, though she hated the piano.

"Don't duck your head in that slouchy way, Alicky," her mother said. "I don't know why you young people are getting so slouchy these days. Stand straight like a princess. Well, run along, both of you. What are you waiting for?"

And Alicky and I went off together, slouching when we were out of sight.

"I hope I'm like your mother and not my mother when I grow up," Alicky said. "I don't want to be bossy like that. Let's go to the orchard."

"Why not the brook?"

"I'd rather the orchard. Come along now, Trish."

That visit, as I said, was one of the good ones. The bad ones came later, after my father had lost his job, and my mother and I came uninvited. Now, all these years later, I'm not sure that I blame Uncle Dan and Aunt Alix if they made us less than welcome. I don't like uninvited guests either; and, whatever nostalgic people may say about the Depression, hard times don't make people warmer and more generous. After all, the bite the unbidden guest eats may mean less porridge for your own children. Or was it my imagination, or my mother's imagination, that the food was being measured?

In fact, Uncle Dan and Aunt Alix were more visibly prosperous than before. The new house had been built; and it was larger and more handsome than the old one, but more difficult to heat in winter, so that the room where my mother and I slept was very cold for a December visit. Electricity had only recently been installed, and a naked light bulb hung on a chain over our bed. There was a bathroom also, the pride of the house, so that the old pitcher and basin and chamber-pot were no longer considered necessary; but the flush made loud, violent noises when it was flushed, and there was no hot water in the taps, so that warm water had to be carried upstairs from the kitchen for a bath; a great ceremony that made frequent washing difficult. Perhaps it's because I don't like to be in competition for the bathroom and the breakfast eggs that I don't like now to visit friends and relatives. Hotels are better. In hotels I know I've paid the bill.

The worst visit came the year there was typhoid in the village, the year my mother decided to take a job as housekeeper for a family where there had been typhoid and they could get no-one, so we heard, to work for them. "If you go and work for the Ritchies, Josie," Uncle Dan said, "you needn't come back here. I won't have typhoid in the house."

"The doctor says it isn't catching from person to person, Dan," my mother said. "They must have got it some other way. Mary Ritchie caught it when she was on a visit to Bathurst. From the water, they think."

"I don't care what the doctor said. Doctors don't know everything."

"I just want to be independent," Mother said.

"Be independent, then, and kill yourself and Trish if you want. But don't come crawling back here when you need help."

"I've never crawled," my mother said angrily. "I won't ever crawl." There was a high pink flush on her cheekbones. She got up and beckoned me, and we went off to pack the old suitcase that held her clothes and mine.

Aunt Alix came to our room, waddling heavily. "Change your mind, Josie," she said. "He means it. You know I can't take your part against him." I was surprised by the note of pleading in her voice, which I had never heard before. Mother shook her head, not trusting herself to speak.

Uncle Dan drove us to the Ritchies'. It was a silent quarter-hour drive, and he drove away before we tapped at the Ritchies' door. The woman who came to the door was the new housekeeper, so my mother had no job after all. But she took us into the kitchen, gave us tea and sent us down the road, to the house of a woman who might need someone to help with the housecleaning.

In fact it was several days before Mother found a temporary job, and several nights of sleeping at relatives' houses. But not at Uncle Dan's house.

It was a long time after that before we visited Aunt Alix; not until after the war started; not until after she visited us.

74

Next morning

Breakfast downstairs in the hotel. Nice to have blackcurrant juice and croissants instead of the inevitable toast and orange juice. But I remember when oranges were a treat for Christmas. Even Aunt Alix didn't usually have them. Prunes were the breakfast fruit in winter, or sometimes applesauce made from dried apples. Rhubarb in the spring. Strawberries and blueberries in the summer. (I am lapsing again into nostalgia.)

I remember we spent a week one summer during the war— my parents and I—at Aunt Alix's. By then we were welcome and the old quarrel had been made up. My father was working in the canteen in the Army Camp in Fredericton; I had won a scholarship and was going to university. Uncle Dan and Aunt Alix were alone. The eldest daughter was teaching. Rowena was married and her husband was in the Navy. Hughie and Eddie were both in the Army. Alicky was working in an office in Montreal.

In the morning we went—my mother and father and I— out into a burned-off patch of bush and picked blueberries. Huge red lard-kettles full of them. Aunt Alix made blueberry pie and blueberry duff. In the hot late afternoon, I tiptoed into the cool, darkened parlour, curled up on the couch in the half light with a novel that had Alicky's name—Alexandra Macnair, 1943—written in it. Uncle Dan peered in at me from the doorway. My mother and Uncle Dan had forgiven one another; my father did not know there was anything to forgive, because he had not been told; but I was not entirely forgiving of Uncle Dan myself, I think, although I covered over my lack of forgiveness. "No, don't get up," Uncle Dan said now. "You look like Alicky there. That's the way she spent her whole visit last time, lying there, reading."

"What's Alicky like now, Uncle Dan?" I asked curiously. I

wished she had been there.

"What's she like?" He sounded surprised and puzzled by my question. "Oh, like any other young girl, I guess. Like you, maybe."

In 1944 Cousin Hughie was reported missing, presumed dead. Mother visited Aunt Alix then, of course, but by that time I had left the Province.

I've just telephoned Alicky's office and asked for Miss Macnair. Or should I have said Ms?

Alicky is quite high up, an executive, no mere secretary. She has a receptionist who asks me to hold. "Trish!" Alicky exclaims when I finally reach her. "Where are you? Why didn't you write me and come and stay at my place?"

"Oh," I say vaguely. "You know how it is. I like to be independent." (I realize that I am echoing my mother.)

"You could have been independent. You could have had the apartment to yourself all day, except for the cats. What about lunch? Dinner?"

We have settled on dinner. She is to pick me up at the hotel after work and drive me to her place. I am curious about her. Probably she is curious about me.

Lunch I'm having in a small place in the Colonnade with an old friend who teaches at Victoria College. Academic talk about an archaeological holiday. I am not full of conversation. My mind is on Alicky, and on Aunt Alix and Uncle Dan.

After my father died one of the uncles drove my mother and me out the Macnair Road to see Aunt Alix and Uncle Dan. They were still alone, more noticeably alone because they were visibly older. Aunt Alix had become very lame; she held onto furniture when she walked around the house. Uncle Dan had to be careful since his stroke. He snoozed in the parlour, while Aunt Alix talked to us on the sunporch, which had been added to the house since our last visit. It was full of geraniums and African violets, and Aunt Alix gave my mother a slip from a double geranium and a small pot of pink violets. "He's never got over Hughie's death," Aunt Alix said of Uncle Dan. "I go to Remembrance Day services, but Dan never does. He won't admit it's happened. He thinks Hughie will be back." Of course Hughie never did come back. And now Uncle Dan and Aunt Alix have been dead for years.

The last time I visited Aunt Alix was when my own mother died. Mother had been living with me since my father's death; but we had taken her home to be buried. Before the funeral my sister Carrie and her husband stayed with a younger uncle in the village, but my uncle said, "Your Aunt Alix wants you to stay with her, Trish. She asked specially."

"How is Aunt Alix now?" I asked.

"Failing," he said. "She's nearly 80 now, and she's never got over Dan's death." (I could hear her own words echoing.) "And now Josie's death will be another great blow to her. They were very close, you know that."

I was driven out to Aunt Alix's by Rowena's husband, Orville Hawkins. Orville and Rowena had moved in with Aunt Alix, though Orville worked in an office in town and didn't do much farming. Aunt Alix and Rowena were waiting for me in the kitchen. Aunt Alix half rose from her rocking-chair and took me in her arms. I realized that this was almost the first time she had kissed me. Neither of us cried; but Aunt Alix sat me down opposite her and patted my hand gently. "How did Josie go?" she asked. "Did she suffer much?" She looked very old; and yet, oddly, there was something younger about her than I had ever seen. Rowena was slicing bread and butter, and brought it to us with hot tea. To my surprise I was ravenously hungry, though I felt ashamed of my hunger.

I slept in a room with a candlewick bedspread, like the bedspread in the hotel-room. There was a light swinging on a chain above the bed, but this time the bulb was not naked. I wondered if this was the room where I had slept before with my mother, the times we had felt unwelcome; but of course I couldn't ask Aunt Alix.

I woke in the night, smothering in the pile of feather pillows. Was a ghost stirring? I tried to find the lamp chain, but the room was totally dark, as only a room in the country can be, miles from any streetlights. Finally, after several attempts, I found the chain and pulled it. I tiptoed into the hallway. Aunt Alix's door was open, and she was sitting up in a big chair reading her Bible. She had written in my mother's death, and showed me the page. "There's nobody alive who's known me as long as Josie," she said. "All my life except the first two years. Now there's nobody left who'll understand."

"Tell me about when you and Mother were young," I said.

"Josie danced to the fiddle and was named for an Empress," she told me, "but I was fat Martha with a plain name. But I loved Josie."

"You were both pretty," I said. "She told me so."

"Did she? Perhaps she was right. It's a long time since we were girls, and yet it's just the other day."

She started to tell me about school, about going to school with Josie, and about playing on a rock in the backyard, and about their mother, who wore pink silk to church and a brown cotton dress for housework, and about their little brother who died young, and about growing up and going to picnics and dances. We were both, I was sure, thinking of that day when Mother and I had left the house and Uncle Dan had told us not to come back, but neither of us mentioned it. Aunt Alix, I thought, had done as well as she could, placed between two people she loved. Queen Alexandra, after all, had been a consort rather than a reigning queen like Victoria.

"But you're tired, child," she said, looking at me finally. "You'd better go back to bed. Get some sleep before the funeral."

I got up, reeling with sleepiness. "You both loved each other," I said. The truth. Which didn't mean they didn't envy each other or grudge one another beauty or good fortune, or fail each other at times.

I never saw Aunt Alix after my mother's funeral. She died that summer, in her sleep, while I was out of the country on vacation.

Alicky meets me in the hotel lobby, and we find our way out to her car. I doubt if we'd have recognized each other if we hadn't been looking for each other, although Alicky does faintly resembly her mother. Her long, fair hair is beginning to go grey and she wears it in a roll. Her eyes are blue like her mother's, but appear deepset because her face is so thin; and she is pale rather than pink-cheeked. She is taller than her mother, and angular. Her clothes are tailored and unostentatious, but I am sure they are expensive. Not that mine are cheap, I remind myself.

Her apartment, when we reach it, also looks expensive. It is full of modern, rather chilly furniture and thick carpets. Things match, as they don't in my rather higgledy-piggledy house, where the sideboard is Victorian and the dining-table is just the other day. I politely admire her view, although I really prefer my own view in Edmonton, with its glimpse of the prairie in the distance.

She opens a door and brings out the two cats, which have their own room. There is an apartment rule against cats, but she has broken the rule. The cats are both Siamese, handsome and nervous. They are only distantly related, I think, to the plebeian barn cats that had the run of Uncle Dan's farmyard. Alicky pets them lavishly, and prepares supper for them before turning her attention to ours.

"That's an elegant black dress," she tells me.

"I just bought it," I say, and wonder if I am perhaps over-dressed.

79

Alicky offers me a drink, and I sip a sherry, standing in the doorway of the little kitchen while she busies herself with dinner. We have filet mignon and a salad. "Steak's easy," she says. "I'm afraid I'm not very domestic."

"Neither am I," I tell her. "Not like Mother and Aunt Alix."

"Oh, them. Who has the time now? Well, maybe Rowena does. You know you saw Mother later than I did, don't you? I saw her the Christmas before she died; that was the last time."

We eat in the dining-alcove off the kitchen. The cats have had to be put back in their room because one of them leaped onto the table. Probably they eat there when Alicky doesn't have company.

I tell her about that last time I visited her mother, about the Family Bible. "I suppose you knew her real name was Martha?" I say.

She nods. "It's my middle name, too. As a matter of fact, that's the name I use now. It's better than Alexandra, and Alicky sounds like a colt. Plain names are fashionable again."

Has Aunt Alix somehow been defeated, I wonder? But then she didn't entirely reject Martha as a name, did she?

"Are you going home for Christmas this year? To Rowena's?" I ask.

"No. Last year I went to Vancouver, to see Eddie and his wife. This year I think I'll just stay here with the cats. There's nothing left for me on Macnair Road, really. Would you like to come and stay with me, Trish?"

"Thanks. Carrie expects me this year."

"I've known you as long as Carrie has, haven't I? I'll bet you won't even stay with Carrie, will you?"

I laugh. "No, I'll stay at the hotel and have dinner with Carrie."

"That's what I thought. Not that I blame you, Trish. I know why you don't like to visit. But it's a long time ago now, isn't it? I always liked your visits myself. So did Mother, only maybe she thought Dad didn't. He and your mother were both pretty stubborn, weren't they?"

"You could visit me," I say. "Next time."

"How about that? Yes, I could visit you. Maybe summer would be better than Christmas, would it? Do you think I'll need a passport for Alberta by then?"

"Don't be silly, Alicky—Martha. That's only a family quarrel. Make us some good New Brunswick tea, will you, instead of coffee?"

"Who's being bossy now, Trish?"

She makes the tea and brings it in. Then she goes off and brings back a thick, fat, black book. "Grandmother Darrah's Family Bible," she says. "None of the others wanted it, can you imagine? There was a Macnair family Bible too, and Rowena has that. Would you like to have it? I have no family but the cats. See—mother wrote Aunt Josie's death in that night you talked of, and I wrote Mother's death."

"You keep it," I say. "I'll visit it now and then."

We sit quietly, drinking our tea, as if we were in Aunt Alix's kitchen. Alicky-Martha looks at me thoughtfully with her mother's blue eyes, and I raise the teacup in my mother's hand, with its crooked little finger, inherited in turn from her mother.

her first apartment

And now the caretaker, who had helped her up to the third floor with her two suitcases, flung open her door and there it was. Her own apartment. Her first apartment. From the little hallway you looked right into the living-room with its wide picture window. The morning sunshine poured in, sifted through green leaves beginning to turn gold. Blue walls, like the sky. Blue carpet. (And blue was her favourite colour.) Chesterfield, big stuffed chair, little spindly chair, all looking comfortable in the sunlight.

"You like it?" the caretaker asked.

"Oh, yes," Cass breathed. She couldn't have told him how much she liked it. She was relieved, for one thing, that it was so pleasant. She had rented it sight unseen, and of course even though it was university housing and should be all right, you never knew. And she had spent last night, her first night in Bloomington, in a perfectly awful hotel. She had come first to the apartment building when she arrived in the evening by train, but the caretaker had been off duty, and a student—was he an Arab?—she had met in the hallway had suggested the hotel. "It's cheap," the student had said, "but it's quite good enough. My wife and I stayed there when we came from Egypt. You might as well save money." Well, it had been cheap. Anyhow, here she was, and she hoped she hadn't collected any bedbugs.

"Kitchen's to the right," the caretaker said. The merest doll's kitchen, but it had everything: a little electric stove, a refrigerator, a table with two chairs. The caretaker swung the kitchen cupboards wide for her, to check that there was nothing wrong with the hinges, pointed out a card with "Rules For Tenants" taped to the kitchen wall.

No bedroom, but there was a dressing-room with two chests of drawers. "Lots of cupboard space here," the caretaker waved a hand. And the bathroom beyond that. Everything shining and in order. All hers.

After the caretaker had left (handing her the key—her key) Cass crossed the living-room right away to look out the window. Beyond the trees was the street, with a few shops on the opposite side. Good—there was a little grocery shop. She would go there later, buy a few necessities. She circled the room lovingly, opening and closing the drawers of the desk, tapping the empty shelves of the bookcase, perching momentarily on each of the chairs. The place would look like home once she had a few of her own things about: the little blue bud vase with a glass bubble imprisoned deep in its centre; the old copper candlestick, complete with curving handle, which she

83

had bought in a secondhand store in Halifax; oh, and the small piece of driftwood that her sister had picked up on the beach at Bayfield when they were walking together this summer. It looked like a little whale, Vera had said. It could go on top of the desk.

But she must go out to the kitchen again, turn on stove burners to make sure they worked, open the doors of the empty kitchen cupboards and make a mental list of things she would need. Saucepans. A toaster. A teapot. And of course groceries. Everything. Not all today, of course. Good heavens, how could she ever manage to get all these things?

Standing there on the floor of her own kitchen, she felt the first sinking of her heart, a pang of homesickness. Would she manage by herself? All that distance from home, and in a foreign country too. Of course she had lived away from home before, but in Halifax and Toronto, which were different but not foreign. And before, she had either lived in university residences, where you lined up three times a day for meals on a tray, or, these past two years when she was working at the library in Halifax, in a rooming-house kept by the widow of a Halifax civil servant. Mrs. Barnes had cooked dinner every day for Cass and the other two boarders. Cass had bought lunch at a cafeteria, prepared breakfast for herself in Mrs. Barnes' kitchen. Mrs. Barnes had made real coffee, percolated, but Cass had never got beyond instant. If instant hadn't been invented, she would have had to stick to tea. At home she had never done much cooking. Vera had always been the domestic one.

The door bell buzzed loudly. Her door bell. It was her trunk, which had come through on the train with her and was now being delivered. Good, she would have sheets to sleep in tonight. And she had packed two place settings of her mother's Spode, though Vera, as the elder, and the one who was married, had most of it, now that their mother was dead and their father, who was living alone, didn't need it. She had the man take it into the dressing-room, where she could unpack at leisure.

She hunted in her handbag for her keys, found them. Which one? The first one she tried didn't work. It must've belonged to that old trunk of her mother's she'd had when she went to Toronto, the one that had had a spring broken. And here was the right key. Everything safe. The Spode. Her precious bud vase. Vera's dear little whale, wrapped around with a facecloth to keep him from being damaged. Vera had glued two little black bead eyes on each side of what looked to be the head, and on the whale's tummy she had written, in neat blue ink, "White Whale, Bayfield, NS, August." Just last month. Cass carried him out to the living-room, along with the blue bud vase. She put them both on top of the desk, stood back looking at them with pleasure. Now she was at home. She would do the rest of the unpacking later. First she must buy some groceries, just to make sure of something for tomorrow's breakfast.

In fact, she was hungry now, she thought, preparing to go out, making sure she had her key. A cardigan for her shoulders, perhaps. She certainly didn't need her coat. It was still warm here, warmer than it would be at home. She turned the little button in the door as she went out, made sure it was locked behind her, walked down the three flights of stairs.

This was one of two university apartment buildings, exactly alike on the outside—probably on the inside too, except for whatever small changes the tenants might make. (Books. Driftwood whales.) No pictures were to be hung, she had noticed among the rules. The apartments were Married Students' Housing, but they were also open to Faculty, including unmarried Faculty. And librarians rated—though marginally—as Faculty. That was how Cass was able to have this apartment. Once she had picked up her groceries, she must report for her job. She was supposed to have arrived at the beginning of September; but, because of delays with her visa, it was now the middle of the month. The head librarian had told her it was perfectly all right—come when she could —but the delay had made her nervous.

The grocery store she had seen from the window was small but moderately well-stocked. It was fun to buy groceries for her own kitchen: bread, butter, eggs, cheese, bacon, tea-bags, toilet paper, canned soup, soda crackers, jam, oranges, sugar. Was there a milkman who came to the apartment building, she wondered? She picked up a couple of tins of evaporated milk. Cornflakes. Oh, soapflakes and a cake of soap too. The grocery store had a few household items. She bought a saucepan, a plastic tumbler, plastic knife, fork and spoon, a can opener. Other things could wait until she could manage a trip down town. And she could buy meat and vegetables on her next visit to the store. She would treat herself to dinner out today. Somewhere near the university.

Climbing the stairs, she felt the weight of the bag in her arms, shifted it uncomfortably. Yes, a milkman did come. She saw a bottle of milk just outside someone's doorway, not yet taken in. She must find out....

On the second floor, she met the Egyptian student. "Did you like the hotel I sent you to last night?" he asked.

"Not very well," Cass answered honestly.

"No, but I did save you money, did I not?" he asked, in his careful English. "And now it is over. You should have waited to buy groceries. My wife and I go to the supermarket every week. We could have driven you. It is much cheaper."

"Thank you," Cass said. After the hotel he had advised, she didn't feel disposed to be too friendly. That hotel.

Shutting the door behind her—locking it this time, too— she put the bag of groceries on her kitchen table. She would make herself a cup of tea and eat a slice of bread and butter. No teapot, no kettle, but she could boil water in the saucepan, pour it over the tea-bag in her Spode cup. There—she had managed to jab two holes in the tin of milk, and poured a little into the cup before trusting the boiling water in it. Strawberry jam for the bread. Good. She had been hungry. She hadn't eaten much breakfast because she had wanted to come over here as soon as possible. And to get away from that hotel too, she must admit.

Not that she had minded so much in the morning, with the sun shining. But last night, just after she had arrived in the room, she had felt dismay. They had asked her to pay in advance, too, so she could hardly change her mind and move out.

Well, to be just, the sheets were clean enough. She had probably not collected bedbugs. It was just that it looked like a place where you might collect bedbugs. The room had managed to be both battered and gaudy, with whorish yellow wallpaper, a lamp with a tipsy fringed orange lampshade. There had been a dripping tap in the bathroom. Then a violent, drunken quarrel had begun in the room next door. Apprehensively, Cass had fastened the chain on the door, pushed a chair against it for more security. She had thought she would never sleep, but surprisingly she had.

Of course she had been up early in the morning, had gone next door for coffee and a doughnut (she would not eat at the hotel), had then called the apartment building to make sure the caretaker was in, and had taken a taxi right over with her suitcases. And now, here she was, practically settled in, having her first meal—could you call it a meal?—in her own apartment. But why ever had the student recommended that hotel? She found it hard to forgive him.

It was good that electricity went with the apartment. That was a saving. But she would need to have the telephone connected. She tried it, just to make sure. If it had been

87

connected, she would have telephoned the library. But of course it was dead, as she had expected. Well, she would just have to inquire her way to the library, walk over (she knew it was within walking distance) and announce herself.

And she had forgotten dishtowels. She rinsed her few dishes under the tap, left them on the ledge to dry. She hated to leave the place—her own place—in order to go to work. But the library would be a new place too. She would just let them know she was here, and then she would ask if she could take the afternoon off for shopping.

By the time she returned to the apartment, evening had set in. She had, after all, put in a full afternoon's work. Miss Pyke, the chief cataloguer, had not let her go once she had got her. She had taken her from desk to desk in the big cataloguing room ("Cataloging" the sign on the outside said: she must remember to use American spelling at work) introducing her to people, mostly women, but a few men. "This is Cass Pine, from Canada," she kept saying. "She's going to help catalogue serials for us."

And they would smile and say, "Hi there, Cass," or "Do you come from near Calgary? I have an uncle in Calgary," or "Bet it's cold up there now. I see you've got a jacket on already." It was warm in that room, all right. The women sat in cotton dresses, their hair ruffled by the breeze of the heavy fans that whirred on each counter top. Cass tried to smile back at them, wilting in unaccustomed September afternoon heat, her feet hurting. There was a blister, she knew, on one of her heels. Those new shoes.

After work she had found her way to the Students' Union —air conditioned, thank goodness—and ate a meal off a tray in a solitary corner of the cafeteria: a decent enough Salisbury Steak at a fair price, with a tossed salad to go with it. No special treat, though.

As soon as she stepped inside the door of the apartment, she realized there was something else she needed to buy. There was no light in the living-room. Of course she hadn't noticed in the morning, with all that sunlight pouring in. She must've taken for granted there would be a central light fixture provided, but there wasn't. There were ceiling lights in the kitchen and in the dressing-room and twin lights flanking the mirror in the bathroom; so she wasn't left totally in the dark. But she wouldn't be sitting cosily in her lighted living-room reading the evening paper. Which, anyhow, she hadn't thought to buy. Even a candle for the copper candle-stick would have helped. She spent most of the evening in the dressing-room unpacking, putting clothes on hangers, then taking a long, leisurely bath in the tub. (She had not felt like using the tub at that hotel.) She wished she had a radio. Must buy one. Maybe after her first salary cheque.

And now, how was she to open up the chesterfield? She hadn't thought to ask the caretaker and couldn't seem to work it out. Oh, well, for tonight she would sleep on it as it was. At least she had sheets, and the one blanket she had packed. She had to leave the light on in the dressing-room in order to see her way to bed; and, even so, she managed to crack her shins against the coffee-table in front of the chesterfield. Getting up again, she picked up the little driftwood whale from the desk and brought it over to the bed with her. She lay there stroking it with one finger, as she used to stroke her child-hood teddy-bears. It's not really a whale, she thought. It's a piece of driftwood. But it's just as much of a mystery as a whale would be, isn't it? Laying it on the coffee-table, she closed her eyes and tried to sleep, but for a long time she couldn't. The light from the dressing-room bothered her eyes. She had no pillow, only her folded terry bathrobe, which felt rough against her face. She couldn't hear people, as she had last night in the hotel; but she was conscious of a whole building full of strangers, asleep or awake.

The next morning she opened her eyes early, before her little travelling alarm clock went off. She felt stiff from the cramped position in which she had slept, not really rested. Getting up, she stretched and yawned.

In the little kitchen, she filled the saucepan with water, watched it come to a boil, while she stood in her pyjamas peeling an orange and dipping the sections of the fruit in sugar. Through the walls of the kitchen—above, below?—she heard voices. Married voices, she decided. "And I am not your mother; I never will be your mother," the woman was saying, in high, exasperated tones. Cass coughed, banged a cupboard door. It was only fair to let them know she was here. The man's answering voice was an indistinct mumble. Thank goodness. She drank her instant coffee, ate bread and cheese, wishing for toast. In a week's time, she thought—in two weeks' time—she would be settled in.

2

Cass settles in. Laura Belle Moore, who works in the Education Library and lives on the floor below Cass, shows her how the chesterfield (which she calls the sofa) works. "It's just a simple hide-a-bed," she says. "Quite an easy model, really." She invites Cass down one evening to watch *Annie Get Your Gun* on TV, though Cass doesn't much like TV. The TV doesn't work well in this building, anyway: something about the building, Laura Belle says. All that steel and concrete, maybe. The little radio Cass buys doesn't work well, either, and there isn't much on it. Cass misses Canadian radio, which she thinks is better. She has bought a gooseneck lamp for the desk, and on the end table to the left of the chesterfield (the sofa?) she has placed a white lamp with blue flowers on the base, topped by a blue lampshade. Her little clock sits beside it at night, and the driftwood whale. There is a red candle in her candlestick holder, which is still on the desk.

For the kitchen she has bought a teakettle (not electric—she can't afford that yet), a teapot in the shape of a cabbage, muffin tins, a loaf pan, a pyrex casserole, a frying-pan, the cheapest toaster in the five-and-ten, a slop pail that doubles as garbage tin, canisters for flour, tea, sugar and coffee, four each of stainless steel knives, forks and spoons, and four quite pretty white bread and butter plates with a delicate lacy edge, on sale by an unnamed manufacturer because of flaws. She has also bought two cookbooks and is gradually teaching herself to cook. She has worked her way through breakfasts and is now on lunches, though she can do a few simple dinners too.

There are new books in the bookcase, magazines on the coffee-table. She reads a lot in the evenings. Saturdays she shops down town, in the shops in the Square surrounding the courthouse, and has lunch in one of the two hotels: the good hotel, not the one she stayed in that first night she was here. Sunday afternoons she takes long walks through the campus under the dreaming, mellowing trees, through masses of fallen leaves, beside the Jordan River, as the brook that flows through the campus is named. It is a slow, gentle autumn of soft blue skies and sunshine yellow and cloying as honey; not sharp, frosty, flamboyant, like the fall she is used to at home.

She is unspeakably lonely at first, writes long letters to Bayfield, Halifax, Toronto, saying how much she likes the place, but would Vera, would her father, her cousins, her friends write right away?

Then, gradually, she makes a few acquaintances. There is the Egyptian student, of course, who comes to see her with his wife. The wife can't speak English and has to have everything translated to her by her husband. They take Cass once to the supermarket for shopping, but she likes the little corner grocery better, and manages to avoid going with them again. She is pleased to discover that she can buy a bottle of sherry at the grocer's, and keeps some on hand to offer company if they ever come. A woman from the Welcome Waggon finds her, rather late, and brings her coupons from the shops down town. (That is one of the few evenings when Cass has been too tired to make up the hide-a-bed from the night before. The room is a mess.) It is the woman from the Welcome Waggon who sends Angie Travis to see her. Angie is from England, has just come out on a year's appointment to teach in the Geography Department. She is a sturdy-looking young woman with dark curling hair and no makeup, wearing tweeds and sensible shoes. She is older than Cass—perhaps 30. She wanders around Cass' apartment on her first visit, says, "We have exactly the same flat, except mine's rose and yours is blue. But you've made yours quite homely. I say, what an interesting piece of driftwood. Quite phallic, isn't it?"

Angie tells Cass that she has given up being domestic this year, is living on coffee and bananas. Cass thinks that at least she can do as well as that, and invites Angie to dinner. She serves her a carefully constructed meatloaf, a tossed salad made in imitation of those served at the Students' Union, instant mashed potatoes, peas from a box of frozen peas and canned fruit cocktail with ice cream. Angie eats it cheerfully and says it is very good. She doesn't seem to mind that the coffee is instant. "Civilized cups, too," she says, looking at Cass' Spode, which she is able to use because there are only two of them.

It is Angie who introduces her to the Prossers, Gareth and Olwen. Cass is fascinated by the Prossers. They are brother and sister, not twins, but within a year or so of one another in age. They are striking looking, with dark eyes and hair and thin, dark profiles looking, Cass thinks, like the people on antique coins she has seen represented in books. Olwen dresses beautifully, in clothes that are fashionable and yet have something just faintly medieval about them. The Prossers are Welsh, but have lived in many places. In Greece. In

92

India. In Egypt. Gareth is teaching here now in the Classics Department, and Olwen has some job, some office job. She waves it away with her hands when she speaks of it. She has graceful hands, long and white. Cass invites the Prossers to tea with the Egyptian student and his wife, but Gareth and the Egyptian do not take to each other, she can see. Next time she will invite them separately, or with Angie.

Angie is writing something in her spare time. She is mysterious about it at first. Cass decides she must be writing a novel. But no. What she is writing, she finally tells Cass, is an account of her psychoanalysis.

"Have you been psychoanalyzed?" Cass asks, surprised. Angie seems so normal—almost abnormally normal. "Was something the matter?"

"Everything," Angie says, darkly.

What had been the matter, Cass gathers, was Angie's mother. The father hadn't counted; he and the mother had separated when Angie was a small child. Now Angie almost doesn't remember him.

"It's mothers who always cause the trouble," Angie says. "They dominate."

"Do they?"

Cass remembers quarrelling with her own mother, but now that her mother is dead she misses her. Her mother would have written to her more often than her father does. Though he does send her clippings from the Nova Scotia papers, comments on local politics, weather forecasts. (He's always interested in weather. Ever since Cass was a child, he has kept a notebook in which he has jotted the high and low temperatures for the day. So he knows what to expect and when the weather's unusual.) If she were to have a nervous breakdown, she thinks, she doesn't know who she'd blame. Neither of her parents. Herself, maybe. Or Vera, for being older and doing everything first.

93

Gareth and Olwen have an extra ticket to a play and invite Cass to go with them. It's *The Tempest,* with Prospero in his magic garment, Miranda marvelling at Ferdinand and the villains. Cass sits between Gareth and Olwen, is almost equally conscious of them both. Gareth, she thinks, looks Byronic, but is Byron without the club foot. Olwen is wearing a green dress with a silver stole, a silver bracelet on her arm. There is some sympathy between brother and sister that circles them like a bracelet; and tonight she is included in the circle.

After the play they go back to the Prossers' apartment. Gareth opens a bottle of some wine that fizzes. Olwen makes toast for them, and they sit on the floor in the living-room, eating toast with cheese and drinking wine, talking about the play. "Miranda's so innocent she's incredible," Gareth says.

"I don't know," Cass says. "Living alone with her father and Ariel like that." She thinks, for some reason, of the shore at Bayfield, of her father and Vera and Vera's husband Tom. The wind and the waves. Rough magic.

"There was Caliban, too, don't forget," Olwen says. "I could go for Caliban. Simple, direct, a child of nature."

"An oaf and a potential rapist, like most children of nature," Gareth says. "You know you prefer civilization, even if it's decadent, Olwen."

"I suppose I do. I wonder what they were like, Miranda and Caliban, after ten years of decadent civilization in Milan or Naples. I'd have liked to meet them then."

Cass feels they are talking around her, but she likes being here with them. The wine makes her giddy, then drowsy. She sits admiring them both, the dark, handsome brother and sister who look so much alike. There is some mystery about them, she thinks, a mystery she rather enjoys.

"My mother," Angie tells Cass, "is a lesbian. That's why her marriage broke up." They are sitting in Cass' living-room

94

drinking sherry.

"Do you know that, or do you just suspect it?" Cass asks her.

Her own family, she thinks, is so ordinary there's no point talking about them.

"Know? I know it in my bones," Angie says. "It's one reason I turned against her, aside from the fact she's dominant. That's why I don't want to cook or be domestic: because she wants me to."

Cass feels at a loss. There is some jump in thought here that she can't understand. What has being domestic to do with being a lesbian?

She decides to change the subject. "I went to *The Tempest* the other night with Gareth and Olwen," she says. "Did you go to it?"

"Gareth and Olwen," Angie says. "They're a strange couple. Brother and sister, but they share a one-bedroom apartment."

"Olwen has the bedroom," Cass says. "Gareth sleeps on the sofa. They told me."

"You are an innocent," Angie says pityingly. "Why do you think they needed to tell you that?"

Cass wonders if Angie's psychoanalysis has been good for her. But could she possibly be right?

In November, Cass sprains her ankle and twists her foot. The accident happens at work, and when she gets up in the middle of the afternoon to take a coffee break she can't step on the foot. Rebecca Herries, who has the desk next to her at work, drives her to a doctor, who tapes it and sends her home for a week. Rebecca brings her to her apartment building; and, as there is no elevator, the caretaker and the Egyptian student, who appears suddenly on the stairway, carry her up to her apartment. Rebecca prepares dinner for her, pulls out the hide-a-bed, and promises to look in on her in the morning on her way to work. Cass lies miserably in bed, the foot propped up on a pillow, her ankle throbbing and aching. The wife of the Egyptian student comes in and washes her plate and cup for her, nodding at her encouragingly. Her charming little apartment now seems a prison.

It is some time before she can do more than hobble. After her week at home, sitting propped up in her big chair writing letters and reading the opening chapters of Angie's account of her psychoanalysis, she goes back to work; but at first she cannot walk to the library. Rebecca and Laura Belle take turns driving her morning and evening. Rebecca, whose husband teaches linguistics, takes her home to dinner with her husband and daughter, who is in her freshman year at the university (she calls it "School"). Cass enjoys the feeling of being in a family, even though she suspects that Angie, when she meets Rebecca, considers her motherly and dominant.

After Christmas she decides to take a graduate class in English in the evening. She is still hobbling slightly as she walks to class. A Shakespeare class, perhaps because of *The Tempest*.

There is another Canadian in the class, a young man from Ottawa named Malcolm Shore who looks, she thinks, rather like Gareth Prosser. He asks her out to coffee in the Union after class and tells her how homesick he is and how much he hates graduate school. But, as they become better acquainted, she wonders why he is homesick. Home isn't that great. His parents hate each other; they hardly speak to each other; he is their only child, burdened by demands for sympathy from both sides. But he enjoyed his undergraduate years at Victoria College, and he has taught high school for a few years and discovered that he enjoys teaching. He dislikes America: "the American passion for facts and footnotes," he says; "American superficiality," he says; "American glibness," he says.

"You're not quite fair," Cass protests, thinking of Rebecca and her husband. Even Laura Belle. "It's Professor Ringer you don't like, isn't it?"

"Ringer and others. Some of Ringer's students. This place."

They go to movies together, his arm rather diffidently around her. They talk over their term papers together. They have pizzas together at a pizza place, and a celebratory dinner at the hotel restaurant down town. They walk through the campus together at night, arm in arm, telling each other their dreams. Waking and sleeping dreams. He comes up to her apartment to see what it's like, and picks up the little whale. "Mighty like a cloud," he says, smiling. Cass decides she is in love with him, and goes back to a high-school habit of writing poems. She knows the poems are silly—she would die, she thinks, if he were to see them. She carefully tears them up and throws them down the incinerator in the apartment building.

She forgets about the Prossers and Angie, though now and then she sees Gareth and Olwen out for a walk together, and once or twice she sees Angie with a man, quite an old, stout man, somebody in the Geography Department perhaps.

Spring when it comes is earlier, more sudden, more fervid than at home. Leaves, grass, flowers grow, thrust upward, burst stickily open with the rapidity of a fast-motion movie. Outside Cass' window, on the branches of one of the trees, birds whose names she doesn't know cheep, twitter, ruffle their feathers, shrug. There is redwood, dogwood, forsythia. Pear blossoms are blown from the branches and litter the ground. There will be magnolia blossoms. There will be roses.

Malcolm Shore comes to see her, and she cooks dinner for him—she is beginning to be a better cook now—and afterwards they sit together on the sofa talking about their assignments, about their families, about growing up. She tells him about Bill Mair, the boy she went out with for a while in

Halifax. Malcolm has had something unhappy in his past that he doesn't want to tell her. There was some girl a long time ago, someone who is now dead. "I'm afraid of being close to anyone," he says. "I'm afraid of betrayal." Of betraying or of being betrayed? He doesn't say.

"I think you're enjoying being mysterious," Cass tells him. She is half impressed by him, half amused.

The moist, warm breath of early summer comes in through the open window. They are drinking sherry together drowsily; the light is dim in the blue-shadowed room. Does she put her head on his shoulder, or does he draw her into his arms? It's hard to remember afterwards which one made the first move. In fact, however, it's Cass who wants him to go further than he does.

Next week she buys a marriage manual and reads it carefully. It manages to make sex unappetizing, much as some cookbooks make food unappetizing. She wonders about getting the pill, but dislikes asking her doctor to prescribe it. Anyhow, how does she know she will need it? Though she does know. She buys a ruffled peach nightdress with satin ribbons and an extravagant white satin dressing-gown.

It is early June, the end of the spring semester. Malcolm is leaving shortly for Ottawa. Before he leaves he spends the night with Cass. She is happy, but surprised that sex is as messy and painful as it is. It's a relief that he uses one of those rubber safes, but it probably hurts more than if he hadn't. Afterwards she is limp, relaxed, lying in the curve of Malcolm's arm. She decides that she likes before and after best.

The next morning is Sunday. They eat toast and marmalade together, holding hands over the kitchen table. They go back to bed again, and this time it's much easier and doesn't hurt at all.

"Why do you always giggle so?" he asks. "Are you laughing

98

at me?"

"It isn't a laugh, exactly," she says, and is surprised, he doesn't know. Doesn't everybody make that sound?

After he leaves, she looks at herself in the mirror and wonders if she looks different, if people will be able to tell. She thinks she looks prettier, but maybe that's imagination.

3

She met Angie in the lobby of the apartment building. "I'm sorry if I've been neglecting you," Angie said. "I've been intending to come and see you, but I've been busy."

"Have you?" Cass asked. "I've been rather busy myself. With my course and everything. Have you been writing your book?"

"My book? Oh, that. No, I've been busy getting engaged. You may have seen me with Howard, the retired head of the Geography Department. We're being married this summer. Next week at the Town Hall, as a matter of fact."

"The retired head? But isn't he much older than you, then, Angie?"

"Well, yes," Angie said. "He's 66. But he says he's as strong as ever—he wouldn't marry a younger woman if he wasn't— you know—capable."

"That's good," Cass said, smiling faintly. Malcolm Shore wasn't older than she was. In fact, he was six months younger.

She went back to her apartment and ran the little Bissell sweeper over her carpet, singing to herself,

> I'd rather marry a young man
> With an apple in his hand
> Than to marry an old man
> With a hundred acres of land.

Marriage, however, she wasn't sure of. She expected a letter every day from Malcolm, now that he had gone away, but it didn't arrive. She hardly bothered to read letters from her father, from Vera, from friends at home. It was impossible to answer them.

Olwen Prosser rang her door bell. She and Gareth were leaving, she said. Would Cass like her African violets?

"Leaving? Where are you going?"

"Texas, this time. Can you see me in a cowboy hat? Gareth and I never like to stay long in one place."

"I'll miss you," Cass said. And, even though she had forgotten about them, she felt a true pang of loss. They might have been friends. Maybe. Though it was hard to think of Gareth and Olwen needing anyone except each other.

"And this is a silly present," Olwen said, "but I brought you a seashell, to go with your driftwood. You can listen to the sea when you're homesick."

Cass used to believe that story when she was a child, though she knew now there was some other explanation. It was a thin sound, like a ghost whispering. She put the shell beside the whale. Perhaps the voice of the sea would comfort him.

She had done well on her one course. Professor Ringer suggested that she might find it worth while to take more courses. Could she work part-time at the library, or perhaps teach part-time instead? She could get another degree, she could have a university career. And she would forget Malcolm, deliberately forget him, since he still hadn't written to her.

Yes, she decided. In the fall she would leave the apartment, move into a room in a university residence. She stayed on in the apartment through the summer, took another course in summer school.

The apartment was not air-conditioned; even with two large fans, which Rebecca lent her and which Cass left running all night, it was unbearably hot. She sat up late at night writing a term paper on *Sense and Sensibility*. She did not bother to make the bed or dust the apartment. Dishes piled up in the sink in which—one morning—she saw a large cockroach. There were black heel marks on the tile of the kitchen floor.

Angie dropped in on her, and looked horrified at the mess. Angie was very domestic, now that she was married and living in a proper house with air-conditioning. Cass cleared a space on the kitchen counter, made instant coffee for them. "Would you like a banana, Angie?" she asked.

"I've gone off them entirely," Angie said. "You should learn to make proper coffee, Cass. American men expect it."

"Who cares about American men?" Cass asked rudely. She almost said, "Who cares about men?" but was afraid Angie might misunderstand.

Angie told her how brilliant Howard was. "He's had such an interesting life," she said. "He's dictating his memoirs into a tape recorder and I'm typing them out." She was not planning to teach next year.

Late in the summer, Cass was sitting in the main reading-room of the library reading after work. Suddenly she looked up and he was there, walking across the room toward her. She didn't believe it, and stared at him to make sure. He pulled up a chair and sat down beside her. "What are you thinking of?" he asked. She felt she was in a dream, and could not speak. "Somebody told me you weren't well," he said.

She looked at his dark, square face leaning over her, the solidity of the hand on the table near hers. "Oh, I'm well, Malcolm. As usual."

"You've lost weight."

"The weather's been hot. I've been working."

People at the next table were looking at them. "Can't we go somewhere to talk?" he asked.

They went across the street to a small restaurant where they sat in a booth and ordered coffee.

"Why didn't you write?" she asked.

"I don't know. Maybe because I wrote a letter once that a girl showed around and laughed at, and I felt a fool."

"Everybody's not alike," Cass said. "I wouldn't have laughed at you. I wouldn't have shown your letters around."

She felt tears coming to her eyes, but shook her head, and managed to hold them back. She couldn't decide whether she believed him or not. Anyhow, she thought, there were always telephones.

He was not, she gathered, planning to come back for the fall semester. He was returning to teaching. This visit was a conclusion, a farewell.

"You're giving it up, then?" she asked. "Your degree and everything?"

"I might as well now as later. I'll never make an academic. Not here, anyway."

"It seems a waste. I don't think it's so very difficult."

"For you, maybe. If you like that kind of thing."

She wondered if she was being judged for liking it. But then, was an academic career what they were talking about? "What about...?" she started to ask, but did not continue.

The coffee in her cup had gone cold. No, she shook her head at the waitress, she didn't want more.

Coming out of the air-conditioned restaurant into the street, they were hit at once by the moist heat. He walked back toward the apartment with her under the wilting trees.

"The trouble is," he said, "I don't feel real. I feel like a dibbuk."

"What's a dibbuk?" she asked.

"A body that's been emptied of its real owner and possessed

by the dead. Or by a demon."

"I think," she said, smiling, "you've been reading too much Edgar Allan Poe. Or somebody."

They stood together outside the apartment building. She did not ask him in, and he didn't suggest meeting again. The Egyptian student, coming out, looked at them curiously as he passed, and nodded.

As Malcolm disappeared back toward the campus, she almost wondered if indeed he was a ghost. Or whatever that other word was.

She stayed up late that night washing dirty dishes, waxing the kitchen floor. In bed she did cry, finally, reaching out for the little whale, washing it with more water.

Twice, in the night, she awoke from disturbed dreams. Once, she dreamed that Malcolm was in the room with her, walking toward her bed; but, when he reached her, his face belonged to someone else and she was frightened. In the second dream, she and Malcolm were honeymooning together in a dingy hotel, rather like the hotel where she stayed her first night in Bloomington. There were two single beds in the room. On the wall was a notice saying, "The management is happy to provide the happy honeymoon couples who stay here with our funeral wreaths."

Waking, she wondered about that dead girl Malcolm had said he loved. She created an image of her ghost in the room a frail, young creature with long fair hair that she combed before Cass' mirror.

It's only a story, she thought. There may never have been such a girl. She herself, at any rate, didn't intend to be a ghost. Not for many years, at least.

She wanted someone without mysteries. Not Malcolm. Not Gareth and Olwen. Somebody she had not yet met. Might never meet.

Impossible, of course.

In late August she moved out of the apartment. Rebecca came over and helped her pack. Cass had already given the African violets to the wife of the Egyptian student. Rebecca was storing dishes and lamps in her basement, since Cass wouldn't need them in residence.

"How things pile up, even in a year," Rebecca said. "You won't need your toaster, I should think, Cass. What about these bookends? And are you taking this little bit of wood with you, or should it go in the garbage?"

"I'm taking it, please, Rebecca." She picked up the piece of driftwood, wrapped it in a scrap of torn peach nightdress with a satin ribbon attached. One of the little bead eyes had come out, and it looked less like a whale. Had it come from a shipwreck, or was it just a piece of floating branch? It would have its being in other rooms, she thought, maybe even in other countries, on other shores.

"There's some sherry in the bottom of this bottle, Cass," Rebecca said, peering into the back of a cupboard. "Shall we finish it off?"

"Yes, let's, Rebecca," Cass said. "If we haven't packed all the glasses."

"Here we are. Two plastic water tumblers. Well, Cass, one for the road. I hope the next place is as happy as this one."

"Oh, I hope so."

And, as she paused on the way out, standing in the doorway looking back on it, with the sun shining in so brilliantly, it still seemed to Cass a beautiful little apartment, as beautiful as any apartment or house or room where she might ever live.